FIVE REASONS YOU'LL LOVE
A KALLE BLOMKVIST

MYSTERY

Move over Sherlock Holmes. Hit the road
Hercule Poirot. Kalle Blomkvist is on the case!

All the thrills of a detective mystery,
but with plenty of laughs too

A twisting turning plot packed with
intriguing clues

Can you see what the evidence is pointing to?

Can K   dnappers?

KALLE'S GUIDE TO
THE WARS OF THE ROSES

The infamous battles of the Wars of the Roses have raged for many summers now between the fearless and devoted knights of the White Roses—Anders, Eva-Lotta, and Kalle (me)—and the inferior, turnip-headed Red Roses—Sixten, Benka and Jonte.

There are no set rules, but there is one main goal: to cause the opposition as much trouble as possible via the following methods.

- Spying
- Springing surprise attacks
- Overrunning headquarters
- Taking hostages
- Writing insulting letters
- Making peace treaties (in order to break them)
- Stealing your opponents' secret documents (and writing masses of them yourselves)
- Most important of all, retaining possession of *the Great Stonytotem* at all costs!

In reality there's no bad feeling at all between the knights of the White and Red Roses, quite the opposite. But battling is just *the best way* to spend the summer holidays. When you're not trying to catch criminals and solve mysteries, of course . . .

OXFORD
UNIVERSITY PRESS

Great Clarendon Street, Oxford OX2 6DP
Oxford University Press is a department of the University of Oxford.
It furthers the University's objective of excellence in research, scholarship,
and education by publishing worldwide. Oxford is a registered trade mark
of Oxford University Press in the UK and in certain other countries

British Library Cataloguing in Publication Data

Data available

ISBN: 978-0-19-274931-4

1 3 5 7 9 10 8 6 4 2

Printed in Great Britain

Paper used in the production of this book is a natural,
recyclable product made from wood grown in sustainable forests.
The manufacturing process conforms to the environmental
regulations of the country of origin.

A KALLE BLOMKVIST MYSTERY

THE WHITE ROSE RESCUE

Astrid Lindgren

Translated by Susan Beard

OXFORD
UNIVERSITY PRESS

'Kalle! Anders and Eva-Lotta! Are you there?'

Sixten stared up at the bakery loft to see if any of the White Roses would poke a head out of the hatch doors and answer his call.

'And if not, why not?' shouted Jonte, when there was no sign of life from the Whites' headquarters.

'Are you really not there?' Sixten asked again, getting impatient.

Kalle Blomkvist's mop of blond hair appeared in the hatch opening.

'Nope, we're definitely not here,' he said, keeping a straight face. 'We're only pretending.'

The subtle irony was wasted on Sixten.

'What are you doing?' he wanted to know.

'What do you think?' answered Kalle. 'Learning to dance the tango?'

'Nothing you did would surprise me. Are Anders and Eva-Lotta there too?' asked Sixten.

Two heads poked out beside Kalle's.

'We're not here either,' said Eva-Lotta. 'What do you want anyway, Reds?'

'We've come over to pulverise you,' Sixten said, affectionately.

'And find out what's going on with the Great Stonytotem,' Benke added.

'Or are you planning to take the whole summer holidays to make up your minds?' Jonte asked. 'Have you hidden it yet or haven't you?'

Anders slid down the rope, the one the Whites used when they were in a hurry to get down from their headquarters in the bakery loft.

'Oh, we've hidden the Great Stonytotem all right,' he said.

He walked up to the leader of the Red Roses, stared him in the face and said very seriously and slowly:

'Near the desolate fortress, the black and white bird builds its nest. Seek it this very night!'

'Get lost,' was all the Reds' leader said in reply to this challenge. But all the same, he led his trusted followers to a quiet spot behind the blackcurrant bushes to have a good think about the 'black and white bird' bit.

'It's a magpie, of course,' said Jonte. 'The Great Stonytotem is hidden in a magpie's nest. A little kid could work that out.'

'Yes, Jonte, a little kid could work that out,' Eva-Lotta called down from the loft hatch. 'Even a little kid like you. That must make you happy, eh Jonte?'

'Permission to go and clobber her?' Jonte asked his leader. But Sixten considered the Great Stonytotem far more important than anything else, so Jonte had to postpone his mission to teach Eva-Lotta a lesson.

'"Near the desolate fortress"—that can only mean the castle ruins,' said Benka, whispering so that Eva-Lotta wouldn't hear.

'In a magpie's nest near the castle ruins,' Sixten said smugly. 'Come on, let's go.'

The baker's garden gate slammed behind the three knights of the Red Roses with such a bang that Eva-Lotta's cat woke up in fright from its afternoon nap on the veranda. The baker stuck his jovial face out of the bakery window and shouted to his daughter:

'How long will it be, do you think, before you bring the entire bakery tumbling down?'

'*Us?*' said Eva-Lotta, insulted. 'Can we help it if the Red Roses charge around like a herd of buffalo? We don't go crashing about like that.'

'Of course you don't,' said the baker, and he held out a tray of very delicious-looking Danish pastries to the considerate knights of the White Roses who didn't bang garden gates.

A few seconds later the White Roses stampeded out through the gate, letting it slam behind them with such a thump that all the petals on the peonies flowering so beautifully in the flower bed dropped to the ground with a sad little sigh. The baker also sighed. What was that Eva-Lotta had said? Something about a herd of buffalo?

On a tranquil summer night two years earlier, war had been declared between the White and the Red Roses. They were now in their third year of battle and neither side showed any sign of wanting to give up. Quite the opposite, in fact: Anders was always saying the Thirty Years' War was a brilliant example to follow.

'If they could keep slugging it out for so long in the olden days, then so can we,' he used to say, enthusiastically.

Eva-Lotta had a more sensible outlook.

'Just think when you're a fat old man in your forties and the local kids see you sneaking along the ditches in search of the Great Stonytotem. They'll think it's hilarious!'

It wasn't a very pleasant thought, being laughed at. Neither was the idea of being forty while there were people younger and happier, and only thirteen or fourteen years old. Anders felt a distinct dislike for those youngsters who would one day take over playing where they played and had their hiding places and fought their battles of the Roses, and maybe even have the cheek to laugh at him. Him, the leader of the White Roses in their glory days, before those snotty-nosed kids were even born!

Anders was worried. Eva-Lotta's words made him realize that life was short and you had to play while you could.

'No one will ever have as much fun as we've had, anyway,' Kalle comforted his leader. 'Those little pipsqueaks will never know anything like our wars between the Red and the White Roses!'

Eva-Lotta agreed. Nothing could compare to the Roses' wars. When they did eventually turn into those sad old forty-year-olds she had mentioned, they would still remember their wonderful summer game. And they would never be able to think of it without recalling how it felt to run barefoot over the Prairie's soft grass on an early summer's evening, how warm and welcoming the water in the little river felt as they splashed across Eva-Lotta's rickety plank bridge on the way to one of their important battles, or how the hot sun streamed through the open hatch doors into the bakery loft, so that even the floorboards in the White Roses' headquarters smelled of summer. Oh yes, those Roses' wars were forever connected to the summer holidays and gentle breezes and clear, bright sunshine! Autumn gloom and winter cold meant an unconditional truce in the battle for possession of the Great Stonytotem. As soon as they went back to school hostilities were postponed, and didn't break out again until the chestnut trees on the High Street were in bloom again, and their end-of-term reports had been handed over to hyper-critical parents to read.

━━◖▌

But now it was summer and the wars of the Roses had burst into action again, just as the real roses had burst into bloom in the baker's garden. Constable Björk, patrolling along Lillgatan, understood immediately what was going on when he saw first the Reds storming past, followed a couple of minutes later by the Whites at the same hair-raising speed, in the direction of the castle ruins. Eva-Lotta just had time to shout: 'Hello, Constable Björk!' before her blonde ponytail disappeared round the next corner. Constable Björk smiled to himself. That Great Stonytotem—to think kids could have so much fun with so little! The Great Stonytotem was in actual fact only a stone, nothing more than a funny little stone, and yet it was enough to keep the Wars of the Roses going. Well, of course, when it came to war, it didn't take much, did it? Constable Björk sighed when he thought about how little it took. Deep in thought, he set off over the bridge to take a closer look at a car that was parked in the wrong place on the other side of the river. Still in a philosophical frame of mind, he walked halfway across the bridge before stopping to stare at the water flowing under the arches. An old newspaper came sailing along on the current. It bobbed gently in the waves and its bold headline would have been the latest news yesterday or the day before, or perhaps even last week. Constable Björk read it, but he wasn't really concentrating.

SUPER-STRONG LIGHTWEIGHT METAL:
REVOLUTION IN THE WEAPONS INDUSTRY
Swedish scientist solves the problem that
has puzzled researchers the world over

Constable Björk sighed again. If only people would limit themselves to battling over the Great Stonytotem, then there would be no need for a weapons industry!

But for now he had an illegally-parked car to see to.

'They'll look in that whitebeam tree behind the castle ruins first,' Kalle said confidently, giving a happy little skip at the thought.

'True,' said Eva-Lotta. 'There's never been a magpie nest like it!'

'And that's why I've put a little note to the Reds inside it,' said Anders. 'They'll go berserk when they read it. I think we might as well stop here and wait for their attack.'

Directly above them, on top of the hill, the crumbling walls of the old ruin rose up against a pale-blue summer sky. It stood there, a brooding old fortress that had been left to decay centuries ago. Far below it were the other buildings of the town, although one or two had hesitantly reached up the steep slope, and drawn closer to the castle on the heights. As the last outpost, halfway up to the ruins, stood an old house partly hidden among the overgrown tangle of hawthorn, lilac bushes and wild cherry trees. A rickety fence surrounded this perfect little retreat. And there, with his back leaning comfortably against the fence, was where Anders decided they would wait for the Reds' return.

'"Near the desolate fortress",' said Kalle, throwing himself down in the grass beside Anders. 'That all depends on how you see it. If we compare the distance between here and the South Pole, we could hide the Great Stonytotem in the area around Hassleholm ten miles away and still say it isn't far from the desolate fortress.'

'You're absolutely right,' said Eva-Lotta. 'We never said the magpie's nest is just around the corner from the castle ruins. But the Reds are such turnip heads, they'll never work that out.'

'They should go down on their knees and thank us,' Anders said. 'Because instead of hiding the Great Stonytotem miles away in Hassleholm, we've hidden it right here by Eklund House. That's really very thoughtful of us.'

'Yes, we are so thoughtful,' laughed Eva-Lotta. And then she said something quite unexpected: 'Look, there's a little kid sitting there on the veranda steps!'

It was true, there really was a child sitting on the

veranda steps. And that's all it took for Eva-Lotta to forget about the Great Stonytotem for a while. Daredevil Eva-Lotta, who was such a courageous warrior, had her moments of womanly weakness—it didn't matter that the leader of the White Roses tried to convince her there was no room for such emotions in the wars of the Roses. Anders and Kalle were always bewildered about Eva-Lotta's behaviour every time she came anywhere near little children. As far as Anders and Kalle were concerned, all little kids were clumsy, snotty and just plain nuisances. But to Eva-Lotta it seemed as if they were adorable little angels, every one of them. When she stepped inside the magical aura of one of these creatures, her stiff, tomboyish figure seemed to soften, and she behaved in a way that was completely dotty, according to Anders. She would stretch out her arms to the child and start talking in a curious cooing voice, which made Anders and Kalle shudder in disgust. The defiant, fearless Eva-Lotta vanished in a puff of smoke. And what if the Reds caught her out at such a moment of weakness? That would be a black mark against the White Roses that they would never be allowed to forget, according to Anders and Kalle.

It seemed the child on the veranda steps had noticed some strange goings-on outside his gate, because he was toddling slowly towards them down the garden path. He stopped dead in his tracks when he saw Eva-Lotta.

'Hello,' he said, shyly.

Eva-Lotta was standing outside the garden gate wearing what Anders called her idiotic smile.

'Hello,' she said, 'What's your name?'

The child stared at her with a pair of serious dark eyes, and didn't seem particularly impressed by the idiotic smile.

'My name's Rasmus,' he said, drawing patterns in the gravel with his big toe. Then he came closer. He stuck a freckly, turned-up nose through the bars of the gate and saw Kalle and Anders sitting on the other side. His serious expression broke into wide grin of delight.

'Hello,' he said. 'My name's Rasmus.'

'Yes, we heard,' said Kalle.

'How old are you?' asked Eva-Lotta.

'Five,' said Rasmus. 'But next year I'll be six. How old will you be next year?'

Eva-Lotta laughed.

'Oh, I'll be a real old lady next year,' she said. 'Anyway, what are you doing here? Do you live here with the Eklunds?'

'No, I don't. I live with my daddy.'

'Does he live here in Eklund House, then?'

'Of course he does,' said Rasmus. 'Otherwise I couldn't be living with him, could I?'

'That's logical, Eva-Lotta,' said Anders.

'Is that her name? Eeba-Lotta?' asked Rasmus,

pointing his big toe at Eva-Lotta.

'Yes, she's called Eeba-Lotta,' said Eva-Lotta. 'And she thinks you're very sweet.'

And seeing as the Reds weren't anywhere in sight, she scrambled over the gate to the sweet child in the Eklunds' garden.

Rasmus couldn't help noticing that here at least was one person who was interested in him, and he decided to be friendly in return. All he had to do was find something to say.

'My daddy makes tin,' he said, after careful thought.

'He makes tin?' said Eva-Lotta. 'What, in a big factory?'

'Course not,' said Rasmus. 'He's a professor who makes tin.'

'Oh, that's nice. Then perhaps he can make some trays for my dad. 'He's a baker, you see, and he needs loads of tin trays to go in the oven.'

'I'll ask my daddy to make one for your daddy,' Rasmus offered, and he put his hand in Eva-Lotta's.

'Come on, Eva-Lotta, don't bother about the kid,' said Anders. 'The Reds will be here any minute.'

'Calm down,' said Eva-Lotta. 'I'll be the first to knock their blocks off.'

Rasmus stared at Eva-Lotta, full of admiration.

'Knock whose blocks off?' he asked.

So Eva-Lotta told him. All about the noble wars between the Red and the White Roses, and the wild chases through the town's streets and alleyways, the dangerous missions and secret orders, and the thrilling snooping about on dark nights. And also about the highly honoured Great Stonytotem, and how the Reds would soon turn up, angry as rampaging bulls, and what a stupendous head-on battle it would be.

And Rasmus understood—finally he understood—the meaning of life. It was to be a White Rose. There could be nothing better. At this precise moment a fierce longing was born deep down in his five-year-old soul to be like this Eeba-Lotta person, and Anders and that other one, whatever his name was—Kalle! To be just as big and strong and knock the Reds' blocks off and give a mighty war cry and snoop about, and all the rest of it. He looked up at Eva-Lotta with eyes brimming with longing, and he said beseechingly:

'Eeba-Lotta, can't I be a White Rose too?'

Eva-Lotta gave his little freckly nose a playful pinch.

'No, Rasmus, you can't,' she said. 'You're not old enough yet.'

That made Rasmus angry. He was filled with righteous indignation when he heard the hateful words 'You're not old enough'. He was always being told that, over and over again. He glared at Eva-Lotta.

'Then I think you're horrible,' he said. After he had made this clear he decided not to bother with her any more. He would go and ask those boys instead if he could be a White Rose.

They were standing by the gate, looking curiously in the direction of the woodshed.

'Hey, Rasmus,' said the boy called Kalle. 'Whose motorbike is that?'

'My daddy's, of course,' said Rasmus.

'Crikey,' said Kalle. 'A professor who rides a motorbike. What a thought. Doesn't his beard get caught in the wheels?'

'What beard?' said Rasmus crossly. 'My daddy hasn't got a beard.'

'Hasn't he?' said Anders. 'All professors have beards.'

'Well, mine hasn't. So there,' said Rasmus, and he stuck his nose in the air and walked back to the veranda. Those children were horrible, all of them, and he didn't want to talk to them any more.

When he reached the safety of the veranda he turned round and shouted at the three people by the gate:

'Bleeping bellybuttons, I think you're horrible! My daddy *is* a professor and he *hasn't* got a beard and he makes tin.'

Kalle, Anders, and Eva-Lotta looked in amusement at the angry little figure on the veranda. They hadn't meant to tease him. Eva-Lotta went to run up and comfort him, but she stopped in her tracks, because at that very second the door behind Rasmus opened and someone came out. It was a suntanned man in his thirties, by the look of him. He picked Rasmus up and hoisted him onto his shoulders.

'You are absolutely right, Rasmus,' he said. 'Your daddy is a professor without a beard who makes tin.'

He came walking down the gravelly path with Rasmus on his shoulders, and Eva-Lotta backed away, because she was on private land, after all.

'See, he hasn't got a beard,' Rasmus shouted triumphantly to Kalle, who was waiting uncertainly by the gate. 'And he *can* ride a motorbike, so there!'

In his head he could picture a daddy with a long beard caught in a wheel, and the thought scared him.

Kalle and Anders bowed politely.

'Rasmus was telling us you make tin,' said Kalle, steering the subject away from the beard business.

The professor laughed.

'Well, I suppose you could call it that,' he said. 'Tin . . . lightweight metals . . . I've made a small discovery, you understand.'

'What kind of discovery?' asked Kalle, interested.

'I've discovered a way of making a lightweight metal super strong and impenetrable,' said the professor. 'That's what Rasmus calls "making tin".'

'Oh, I've read about you in the newspaper,' said Anders. 'That means you're famous!'

'He *is* famous,' confirmed Rasmus from his dad's shoulders. 'And he hasn't got a beard either. So there.'

The professor decided not to discuss what it was like to be famous.

'And now, Rasmus, you and I are going indoors to have breakfast,' he said. 'I'll fry you some bacon.'

'I didn't know you were living here in our town, Professor,' said Eva-Lotta.

'Only for a while,' said the professor. 'I'm renting this old place for the summer.'

'Me and Daddy are having a little summer holiday here because Mummy is in hospital,' said Rasmus. 'Just the two of us, all alone. So there!'

Parents often got in the way when there was a battle to be fought. They interfered with proceedings in many different ways. Sometimes Mr Blomkvist the grocer got it into his head that his son should help out in the shop at busy times. And the postmaster kept coming up with crackpot suggestions for Sixten, such as cutting the grass or sweeping the garden paths. Sixten tried without success to make his father see that an overgrown garden was much more beautiful. The postmaster only shook his head and pointed silently at the lawnmower.

Shoemaker Bengtsson was an even bigger menace. He had been forced to earn his living from the age of thirteen, and he thought his son should do the same. That is why he very firmly tried to keep Anders glued to his shoemaker's stool during the summer holidays. But Anders had come up with a genius method to avoid any attacks on his longed-for freedom. That's why the stool where Anders ought to be sitting was mostly empty when the shoemaker came down into his workshop to teach his oldest son the tricks of the trade.

The only real human being was Eva-Lotta's dad.

'As long as you are happy and behave yourself, and don't get up to too much mischief, then I won't interfere,' said the baker, patting Eva-Lotta's blonde head tenderly.

'Why can't everyone have a dad like that?' Sixten said longingly and very loudly, to make himself heard over the clattering of the lawnmower.

This was the second time in a very few days that his cruel father had made him do the gardening.

Benka and Jonte hung over the fence, staring in sympathy at Sixten's struggles with the mower. They tried comforting him with exaggerated tales of their own problems. Benka had been made to pick blackcurrants all morning, and Jonte had been babysitting his little brothers and sisters.

'If it goes on like this we'll have to spend the nights teaching those Whites a lesson,' said Sixten indignantly. 'I haven't got a single minute free all day, so there's no time to do the important things.'

Jonte nodded in agreement.

'Brilliant idea! Why not do it tonight?'

Sixten immediately let go of the lawnmower.

'You're not so stupid, little Jonte,' he said. 'Come on, let's go to our headquarters and hold a war conference.'

So in their headquarters in Sixten's garage, the Reds planned the night's combat. Afterwards Benka was sent with the Reds' challenge to the Whites. Anders and Eva-Lotta were sitting among the lilac bushes in the baker's garden, waiting for the grocer's shop to close for the day and Kalle to be set free. They were playing noughts and crosses and eating plums to pass the time. In the warm July sun, the leader of the Whites looked sleepy and not especially warrior-like. But he brightened up when he saw Benka balancing over Eva-Lotta's wobbly plank bridge, making the water splash over his bare feet. He was carrying a sheet of paper and he handed over it over to the Whites' leader with a bow, after which he raced off the same way he had come.

Anders spat out a plum stone and read in a loud voice:

This very night by the light of the moon,
the Red Roses will gather
in the fortress of my forefathers,
to celebrate the glorious recapture
of the Great Stonytotem from the heathens.
Warning!!! Do not disturb!!! Every sneaking
little louse of a White Rose will be
cut down without mercy.

Sixten
Knight and leader of the Red Roses.
Note! 12 midnight in the castle ruins.

Anders and Eva-Lotta looked at each other and grinned.

'Come on, let's go and tell Kalle,' said Anders, cramming the note into his trouser pocket. 'This is going to be the night of the long knives, believe me.'

'By the light of the moon' the little town was sleeping deeply and peacefully, with no clue about the night of the long knives. Constable Björk, sauntering along the empty streets, didn't have a clue, either. It was silent everywhere. All he could hear was the sound of his own shoes against the cobblestones. The town slept in the glow of moonlight, and the clear light that shone over the streets and squares gave no hint of the night of the long knives that was to come. But the slumbering buildings and gardens lay in deep shadow, and if Constable Björk had been only a little more attentive he would have noticed a sign of life there in the gloom. He would have noticed the whisperings and the rustling about. He would have heard a window being quietly opened in Mr Lisander the baker's house, and he would have seen Eva-Lotta come out and climb down a ladder. He would have heard Kalle slowly whistle the White Roses' signal over by the Blomkvists' house, and caught a glimpse of Anders before he dashed into the protective shadows of the lilac bushes.

But Constable Björk was weary and longing for his shift to come to an end, and that's why he didn't realize it was the night of the long knives.

The poor unknowing parents of the Reds and the Whites were fast asleep in their beds. No one had thought to tell them about the night's business, but to be on the safe side Eva-Lotta had written a note and left it on her pillow, just in case anyone might notice she was missing. To put their minds at rest she had written:

Hello! Now don't make a big fuss! I've just gone out to fight a battle and I'll be home soon, I think, ha ha ha.
Eva-Lotta

'Just in case of emergency,' she explained to Kalle and Anders, as they climbed the steep hill up to the castle ruins.

The Town Hall clock had just struck twelve. It was time.

'"The fortress of my forefather"—what a joke,' said Kalle. 'What does Sixten mean? As far as I know, there's never been a postmaster living there.'

The castle ruins lay ahead of them in the moonlight, not looking like any post office they had ever seen.

'It's the Reds showing off as usual,' said Anders. 'They need a good sorting out. Not to mention the fact they've got the Great Stonytotem as well.'

In his heart of hearts Anders was rather pleased the Reds had found the right magpie nest and recaptured the Great Stonytotem. One of the ground rules of the Roses' wars was that the precious trophy had to change hands from time to time.

They were quite out of breath after climbing up the steep hill, so they stopped to rest for a minute or so outside the entrance to the ruins. They stood listening to the silence and thinking it looked dark and dangerous inside, under the great archway. Then out from the darkness they heard a ghastly voice:

'Now the Red and the White Roses do battle, and it shall send a thousand souls to death and deadly night!'

A diabolical laugh echoed around the stone walls. And then there was silence, a terrible silence, as if whatever it was that had laughed had suddenly become scared itself of some unknown danger in the darkness.

'To battle and victory!' yelled Anders defiantly, and pelted headlong into the ruins. Kalle and Eva-Lotta followed him.

They had been here many times before in daylight, but never at night. On one memorable occasion they had even been locked in the cellar of the ruined castle. That had been quite nasty, but they thought it was nowhere near as nasty as this—making your way through uncertain gloom in the middle of the night, where anything could be lurking in the shadows. Not only the Reds. No, not the Reds at all, but spooks and spirits, who would take revenge for the interruption of their peaceful night's rest by reaching a knobbly, skeletal hand out of a hole in a wall when they least suspected it, and throttling them. Anders yelled 'To battle and victory' again to lift their spirits, but it sounded so ghastly here in the silence that Eva-Lotta, shuddering, asked him to stop.

'Don't leave me, whatever you do,' she added. 'Because I don't get on with ghosts very well.'

Kalle thumped her reassuringly on the back, and they advanced cautiously. With each step they paused and listened. Somewhere in there, in the darkness, were the Reds. It was their shuffling feet they heard, wasn't it? They hoped so at least. Here and there the moonlight streamed in through the broken roof, and when it did they saw the crumbling walls and the uneven ground as clearly as if it had been the middle of the day. They had to watch out so they didn't stumble. But in places where the moonlight couldn't find a way in there were threatening shadows, creepy darkness and a deathlike silence. And out of the silence, if they listened really carefully, they could make out faint whisperings, fluttery little whisperings that floated into their ears and filled them with horror.

Eva-Lotta was afraid. She slowed down. Who was whispering? Was it the Reds, or was it the fading echo of long-dead voices lingering in the walls? She stretched out her arm to make sure she wasn't alone. She needed to feel the material of Kalle's jacket to protect her from the lurking fear. But there was no jacket and no Kalle, only a black emptiness. Eva-Lotta shrieked in terror. Then an arm came out of a deep niche in the wall and caught her in a suffocating grip. Eva-Lotta screamed. She screamed because she thought her last minute had come.

'Shut up,' said Jonte. 'You sound like a fog horn.'

Dear old Jonte! All at once Eva-Lotta felt enormously fond of him. They tussled silently and energetically in the darkness.

She wondered where on earth Anders and Kalle had got to. But then she heard her leader's voice from a distance:

'What are you screaming for, Eva-Lotta? And where is that celebration, exactly?'

Jonte wasn't all that strong, and Eva-Lotta's small, hard fists soon got her free. She hurtled along the dark passageway as fast as she could, with Jonte right behind her. Someone was coming from the opposite direction now, and Eva-Lotta hit out wildly on all sides to stop herself being caught. But this enemy was stronger. Eva-Lotta felt her arms held in a tight grip—that would be Sixten, of course—but Eva-Lotta certainly wasn't going to give in without a fight. Oh no, not her!

She tensed every single muscle in her body and head-butted him under the chin.

'Oof!' yelled her opponent. It was Kalle's voice.

'What's wrong with you?' said Eva-Lotta. 'What are you fighting for?'

'What are *you* fighting for, when I came to help you?' said Kalle.

Jonte sniggered and ran away from his dangerous companions. He most definitely didn't want to be alone with two White Roses in a dark passageway. He bolted off as fast as he could towards the light opening which led to the castle's courtyard, and as he ran he called back:

'Good idea! Give yourselves a good beating and save us the trouble!'

'After him, Eva-Lotta!' shouted Kalle, and together they ran down the passageway.

But out in the courtyard the two leaders had already met and were locked in combat. They battled in the moonlight, each armed with a wooden sword. Eva-Lotta and Kalle shivered in excitement as they watched the black shadows dodge and leap about. Oh, this was a true War of the Roses! It was precisely here, inside these ancient medieval walls, that fighters ought to meet in night-time combat. This was what happened of course when the real Wars of the Roses were raging and a thousand souls were sent to death and deadly night! Like a nasty, chill little gust of wind, the thought swept through their minds of what it must have been like when the Wars of the Roses was something other than just a good game. Because all of a sudden this moonlit duel didn't feel like a game. It was a battle of life and death, which could only end when one of the black shadows, which were now chasing each other up and down the walls, eventually fell still, never to move again.

'A thousand souls . . .' Kalle whispered to himself.

'Oh, do be quiet,' said Eva-Lotta. Her eyes were fixed on the sword-fighting shadows and she was jumping up and down with excitement. A short distance away stood Benka and Jonte, watching the battle just as breathlessly. The shadows went in to attack, fought hand to hand with their swords, backed off and then went to attack again. All in complete silence, apart from the terrifying clash of the swords as they met.

'Send him to sleep with the lullaby of the sword,' shouted Benka. 'And fight until the fur flies,' he added, in an effort to break the eerie trance he was locked in by the gliding shadows.

That made Eva-Lotta wake up from her trance too, and she took a deep breath to free herself from it. It was only Anders and Sixten fighting with a couple of wooden swords, for crying out loud!

'Drive him out of his forefather's fortress!' Kalle shouted encouragingly to his leader.

The leader did what he could. He didn't exactly succeed in driving Sixten out of his forefather's fortress, but with sharp thrusts of his sword he drove him back to the water pump in the centre of the courtyard. Beside the pump was a fountain in a shallow pool filled with muddy water. And things took a turn for the worse for the Reds' leader when he took a careless step backwards and slithered into the pool.

Kalle and Eva-Lotta's shouts of joy drowned out the Reds' indignant protests. But Sixten clambered out of his unexpected bath—and now he was angry. He set off towards Anders like an angry bull, and just for a change Anders decided to turn and flee. Spluttering with laughter he hared over to the castle wall and began to climb. But before he had time to haul himself up, Sixten had started climbing after him.

'Where do you think you're going?' teased Anders, looking down at his pursuer. 'Off to the banquet in your forefather's fortress, are you?'

'Not before I've ripped your hair out,' Sixten told him.

Anders ran nimbly along the top of the rampart, but all the time he was wondering what would happen if Sixten caught up with him. Fighting up here could be suicidal because on one side of the rampart was a gaping abyss. All Sixten had to do was drive him twenty metres in an easterly direction and there would no longer be a gentle grass slope at the foot of the low wall he was balancing on, but a terrifying drop of at least thirty metres. There was nothing stopping Anders from jumping off the wall before he got that far, but he had no intention of doing that. Danger could be fun, and this night was made for danger. Perhaps some kind of full-moon madness had come over him, because he felt a crazy desire to do things that were extremely reckless. He wanted to do things that would make the Reds gasp.

'Come on then, Sixten,' he taunted. 'What about taking a little moonlight stroll together?'

'I'm coming, don't you worry,' growled Sixten. He knew what Anders had in mind, but it took a lot to make Sixten gasp in amazement.

The top of the rampart was about twenty centimetres wide and no problem at all for anyone used to balancing on a bar in the school gym.

By this time Anders had reached the eastern corner. There was a small round platform here, and then the wall turned south and ran above the steep drop.

Anders took a couple of tentative steps. At that moment he heard the voice of reason inside his head, and it still wasn't too late to obey it. Should he, or shouldn't he?

Sixten was worryingly close by now, and he grinned in delight when saw Anders hesitating.

'Here I am, coming to see the colour of your blood,' he said, in a friendly voice. 'Not afraid, are you?'

'Afraid?' repeated Anders, and he wasted no more time thinking. With a couple of leaps he was out on the rampart wall again. Now there was no going back. He had to balance at least fifty metres above the steep drop. He tried not to look down, and instead stared straight ahead along the top of the wall that stretched out in front of him like a silver ribbon in the moonlight.

A very long silver ribbon—and narrow! All of a sudden so scarily narrow! Was that why his legs were feeling strangely wobbly beneath him? He really wanted to turn round to see where Sixten was, but he didn't dare. And it wasn't necessary, either, because now he heard Sixten's breathing right behind him. Quite nervous breathing it was too. So, Sixten was scared. As for Anders, he was petrified. There was no point denying it. And there, back at the round platform, were the other Roses. They had also climbed up. They were standing there, staring in horror at the crackpot antics of their leaders.

'Here I come . . . to see . . . the colour of your blood,' muttered Sixten, but his bloodthirsty threat didn't sound as convincing as before.

Anders had a think. He could always jump down into the courtyard, of course, but that was still a drop of three metres or more onto a rough stone floor. You couldn't slide down slowly and carefully, because before you started sliding you had to crouch down here on the rampart, and Anders didn't feel like crouching down directly above a vertical drop. No, all he could do was carry on, and not take his stinging eyes off the round platform over there in the opposite corner, where he would be safe.

Perhaps Sixten wasn't as scared as Kalle. At least, he hadn't lost his macabre sense of humour. Anders heard his voice behind him.

'I'm getting closer,' he said. 'I'm getting closer and soon I'll trip you up. That'll be fun.'

It wasn't meant as a threat to be taken seriously. But for Anders it proved disastrous. The very thought that someone behind him would trip him up terrified the life out of him. He half turned, and began to wobble.

'Watch out!' shouted Sixten anxiously.

Then Anders wobbled again . . . and from the corner came a loud cry, because to their absolute horror the White Roses saw their leader plunge head first over the wall.

Eva-Lotta shut her eyes. Desperate thoughts whirled through her head. Where, oh, where was there someone who could help them . . . who would go and tell Mrs Bengtsson that Anders had fallen to his death . . . What would her parents say?

Then she heard Kalle shout:

'Look! He's hanging in a bush!'

Eva-Lotta opened her eyes and stared fearfully down over the edge. Sure enough, there was Anders. A bush had taken root in a crevice a little way down the castle wall, and very conveniently caught the Whites' leader as he came tumbling down to his certain death.

Eva-Lotta couldn't see Sixten at first. The shock had made him fall too, but he had enough wits about him to fall inwards into the courtyard. His hands and knees were cut and scraped, but at least he was alive.

The question was: could Anders be saved? That bush was pitifully small and it sagged worryingly under his weight. How long would it be before it came loose and took off on a little journey down into the depths, with Anders as its passenger?

Eva-Lotta whimpered.

'What shall we do? What on earth shall we do?' she said, staring at Kalle, her eyes dark with despair.

As always, Master Detective Blomkvist took command when danger threatened.

'Hang on, Anders!' he yelled. 'I'll get some rope.'

Only last week they had been practising lassoing here in the castle courtyard. The rope should still be lying about somewhere, with any luck.

'Hurry up, Kalle,' shrieked Jonte, as Kalle tore out through the castle gate.

'Quick, quick!' they all shouted, although that was an unnecessary order because Kalle couldn't go be going any faster.

All the while they were trying to comfort Anders.

'Keep calm,' Eva-Lotta said. 'Kalle will be here soon with the rope.'

Anders needed all the comfort he could get. His situation was pretty unpleasant. He had managed to pull himself up slowly into a sitting position, and here he was, riding on the bush like a witch on a broomstick. He didn't dare peer down into the depths below. He didn't dare shout. He didn't dare move. All he could do was wait. In despair he looked at the bush. The roots were bending and the bark was breaking off in strips. He could see the white fibres inside, twisting and cracking. If Kalle didn't get here soon, there would be no need for a rope.

'Why isn't he coming?' sobbed Eva-Lotta. 'Why can't he hurry?'

If only she knew how much Kalle was hurrying. He darted around like a demented wasp, searching everywhere. Searching, searching, searching . . . but there wasn't any sign of the rope.

'Help,' whispered Kalle, frantically.

'Help,' whispered Anders, his lips white, as he sat on the bush whose life expectancy was suddenly about to be cut short.

'Oh no, oh no!' said Sixten, up on the corner platform. 'Oh no, oh no!'

But then—at last—Kalle turned up, and he was carrying the rope.

'Eva-Lotta, you stay up there and keep watch,' he commanded. 'You others come down here.'

Now they have to act fast. Kalle knows what he has to do: look for a stone to tie on one end of the rope and then throw it over the wall, hoping the stone doesn't hit Anders on the head. Hope and pray that Anders can grab the end before it is too late.

Hands and fingers are so clumsy when there is little time. So horrendously little time.

Below them Anders is staring desperately up towards the wall. Isn't rescue on its way soon? Yes, it's coming. The rope is flung over the top of the wall. But it's too far away. His hands can't reach it.

'Over to the right more,' yells Eva-Lotta from her lookout.

Kalle and the others, in the courtyard below, heave and tug on the rope, trying to get it closer to Anders. But it's not working. It seems to have fastened on something jagged up at the top.

'I can't bear it,' whispers Eva-Lotta. 'I can't bear it.'

She watches the boys as they struggle unsuccessfully with the rope. She sees how helpless Anders is. And she sees the bush bending more and more over the vertical drop . . . Oh, Anders, the whitest Rose of all, leader of the White Roses!

'I can't bear it another second!'

On her naked feet she dashes out onto the wall. Courage, Eva-Lotta! Don't look down, just run over to that rope, kneel down, yes, yes, kneel down, even though your legs are shaking, untangle it and move it, turn around on the narrow wall and run back to the platform.

She does, and then bursts into floods of tears.

And Kalle lowers the rope. The stone dangles in front

of Anders. Slowly, slowly he reaches out for it. The bush bends lower and lower and Eva-Lotta buries her head in her hands. But she was supposed to be keeping watch! She must force herself to look ... now ... now ... Now the bush gives way, it's roots can't cling on in the crevice any longer. Eva-Lotta catches sight of something green floating slowly down and disappearing. But at the very last second Anders grabs hold of the rope.

'He's got it,' she shrieks wildly. 'He's got it!'

Afterwards they stand in a ring around Anders, and feel very fond of him and are so happy he didn't follow the bush down into the depths. Kalle reaches out and touches his arm. He's a good pal, Anders is—and it's good he's still alive!

'It didn't turn out so well for the bush,' comments Eva-Lotta, and everyone laughs hysterically. It is actually hilarious that it didn't turn out so well for the bush.

'What were you doing in that bush, anyway?' said Sixten. 'Looking for birds' eggs?'

'Yes, I thought you might like a couple of scrambled eggs for the celebration in your forefather's fortress,' says Anders.

'But you nearly turned into scrambled eggs yourself,' said Kalle, and they all laugh a lot at that. Ha, ha, Anders very nearly did become scrambled eggs.

Sixten slaps his knees and laughs more than anyone.

Then he realizes his scraped knees are hurting. And he is freezing cold in his wet clothes.

'Come on, Benka and Jonte, let's clear out of here!'

Sixten jogs off towards the courtyard entrance and his faithful team follow after him. In the archway he turns around and waves smugly to Kalle and Anders and Eva-Lotta.

'Cheerio, White Roses, you pathetic little squirts,' he yells jubilantly. 'Tomorrow we'll wipe you off the face of the planet!'

But the leader of the Red Roses is mistaken. It will be quite some time before the Roses meet in battle again.

3

The three White Roses wandered home, happy and contented. It had been a rewarding night and the adventure with Anders hadn't upset them too much. They had the enviable ability of the young to live for the moment. While Anders was clinging desperately to the bush they were scared stiff, but what was the point of being afraid after it was all over? It had ended well, hadn't it? And Anders didn't seem to be suffering from any after-effects in the slightest. He wasn't planning on having nightmares over the little incident. He was planning to go home and have a good night's sleep, trusting that he would wake up tomorrow to a day full of new dangers.

But the Fates had decided that none of the White Roses would get any sleep that night.

They walked in single file along the narrow path back towards town. They weren't particularly tired but Kalle gave a huge yawn and said that the business of sleeping at night had proved really popular in some places, and they could perhaps give it a try some time to see what they thought of it.

'I bet Rasmus likes it,' said Eva-Lotta tenderly, as they stopped outside Eklund House. 'Oh, he must look so sweet when he's asleep!'

'Oh no,' said Kalle. 'Don't start that again, Eva-Lotta.'

Yes, Rasmus and his dad were probably fast asleep in their isolated house at this hour. An upstairs window was open and a white curtain fluttered as if it was waving at the three night wanderers on the path outside. It was so still, so quiet, that Anders instinctively lowered his voice so as not to wake the people sleeping behind that fluttering curtain.

But there was someone else who wasn't quite so considerate when it came to letting people sleep. Someone arriving by car, whose rumbling approach was getting louder through the silence. They could hear the gears grate as it climbed the hill, and then they heard it brake with an angry crunch.

'Who the heck would be driving out here at this time of night?' said Kalle.

'None of your business,' said Anders. 'Come on, what are we hanging about here for, anyway?'

Deep down in Kalle's soul, the sleepy Master Detective stirred.

There were times when Kalle wasn't Kalle at all,

but Master Detective Blomkvist, the brilliant and unstoppable protector of public safety, who divided people into two main categories: 'arrested' and 'not arrested yet'. But Kalle had grown more sensible through the years and now the times when he felt he was Master Detective were few and far between.

But this was one of those times. This was absolutely one of those times.

The person driving that car, where was he heading? There was only one house up here, Eklund House, standing like a solitary outpost far above the town's other buildings. It didn't look as if the professor inside was expecting visitors—the house was sleeping. Could it be a couple in the car, coming up here for a bit of smooching? A couple totally unfamiliar with the area, in that case, because the usual place was in the opposite direction, and you would have to be potty about each other to drive up this winding, hilly road for a bit of smooching in the dark. So who is it in the car? No true detective could allow that question to go unanswered. It was quite impossible.

'Can't we wait a minute to see who it is?' said Kalle.

'Why?' asked Eva-Lotta. 'Do you think it's a midnight murderer on the loose?'

She had hardly finished speaking before two men appeared by the front gate of Eklund House, no more that twenty-five metres away. They could hear the gate squeak softly on its hinges as the two men opened it slowly and walked in. Yes, they walked in!

'Get down in the ditch!' Kalle whispered suddenly, and the next second they were sitting with their noses poking over the top of the ditch, just enough to see what was happening in the professor's garden.

'Well, I expect the professor has invited them,' whispered Anders.

'That's what you think,' said Kalle.

If these really were guests of the professor, they were acting very strangely indeed. If you are someone's guest you don't sneak around as if you are afraid of being discovered. You don't walk round and round the house, you don't test the doors and windows. A welcome guest who finds the house locked doesn't put a ladder under an open window and climb in that way.

But that was what these two night visitors were doing.

'I think I'm going to die,' panted Eva-Lotta. 'Look, they're actually climbing in!'

And that's exactly what the visitors were doing, no doubt about it, if they could believe what their eyes were telling them.

They lay there in the ditch, staring anxiously at the open window and the flapping curtain. An eternity passed. An eternity of silence with no other sounds except their worried breathing and the soft rustle of the dawn breeze in the cherry trees.

Eventually one of the two visitors came out onto the ladder again. He was carrying something in his arms. What on earth was it?

'Rasmus,' whispered Eva-Lotta, and her face turned pale. 'Look, they're kidnapping Rasmus.'

No, that wasn't possible, thought Kalle. Things like that simply didn't happen. Not here. In America, maybe —he had read about it in the papers—but not here.

Apparently it could happen here. It really was Rasmus the man was carrying. He was holding him gently in his arms, and Rasmus was sleeping.

When the man and his burden had disappeared through the gate, Eva-Lotta burst into tears. She turned her deathly pale face to Kalle and whimpered, like she had when Anders was hanging in the bush:

'What shall we do, Kalle? What shall we do?'

Kalle was far too shaken to give a sensible answer. He ran his fingers nervously through his hair and stuttered:

'I don't know... We... we've got get Constable Björk... We've got to...'

He struggled fiercely to overcome the awful paralysis that stopped him thinking clearly. Something had to be done, and fast. But he wasn't able to work out what that could be. They would never have time to fetch the police, he could work that out for himself, at least. The villains would have time to kidnap a dozen kids before the police arrived, and anyway...

The man who had taken Rasmus was coming back. But now he wasn't carrying Rasmus.

'Left him in the car, of course,' whispered Anders.

Eva-Lotta answered with a muffled sob.

They watched the movements of the kidnapper, wide-eyed. To think there could be such despicable people . . . the swine!

The veranda door opened and the man's accomplice came into sight.

'Get a move on, Nick,' he called on a low voice, 'We've got to get this over and done with as quick as we can.'

In a few strides the man called Nick was on the veranda, and they both disappeared into the house.

Kalle sprang to life.

'Come on,' he said, nervously. 'We've got to kidnap Rasmus back!'

'If there's time,' said Anders.

'Yes, if there's time,' agreed Kalle. 'Where do you think the car is?'

It was parked nearby, on the hill. They rushed over to it, running along the ditch as quietly as they could, and they felt incredibly triumphant at the thought of rescuing Rasmus from the hands of the villains. Incredibly triumphant and incredibly afraid.

At the very last second they noticed someone was keeping a watch on the car. There was a man standing on the other side of the road. But as luck would have it he turned his back to them for a moment, and quick as lightning they were able to hurl themselves behind some bushes. They were just in time. The man must have heard a sound that alarmed him, because he whipped round and crossed over to their side of the road. He stood there, staring suspiciously right at the bushes where they were hiding. Could he really not hear their hammering hearts and panting breath?

It seemed a miracle that he couldn't. He stood and listened for a while, then walked round the car and looked in through a side window. Then he paced nervously up and down the road. He came to a halt from time to time and stared towards the house. Perhaps he thought his partners were taking too long?

But there was despair behind the bushes. What could they do while that man was walking about out there? Eva-Lotta cried and Kalle had to nudge her roughly to make her shut up, and also because it wasn't helping his own anxiety.

'Jeepers,' said Anders. 'What are we going to do?'

Then Eva-Lotta swallowed a sob and said briskly:

'I've got to get to Rasmus in the car. If he's going to be kidnapped, so am I. He's not going to face a load of kidnappers on his own when he wakes up.'

'Yes, but . . .'

'Don't talk,' said Eva-Lotta. 'Go and make a suspicious noise in that bush over there, so he forgets the car for a while.'

Anders and Kalle looked at her in horror, but they saw she had made up her mind. And when Eva-Lotta made up her mind, they knew from experience that nothing would change it.

'Let me do it instead,' begged Kalle, but he knew already it was a waste of time.

'Go!' said Eva-Lotta. 'And hurry up!'

They did as she told them, but before they disappeared they heard her whisper behind them:

'I'll be like a mum to Rasmus. And I'll leave a trail after me, if I can. You know, like Hansel and Gretel.'

'Good,' said Kalle. 'And we'll follow you like two bloodhounds.'

They gave her a wave of encouragement and tore off silently through the bushes.

How good it is on occasions like this to have a gift for creeping about silently! Not for nothing had they been taking part in their Wars of the Roses for such a long time. They'd had plenty of practice in capturing lookout positions. Like that oaf on the road, for example! He was supposed to be keeping an eye on Rasmus, those were his orders. But here he is, pacing up and down between the car and the house. Up and down, up and down. And then he hears a suspicious crackling in that bush over there, and of course he has to go and investigate. He leaps over the ditch and plunges into the tangle of hazel bushes. Oh yes, very much on his guard and very watchful! But it was the car he should have been guarding, the buffoon! All sorts of things could be going on at the car while he's investigating the hazel bushes. A complete waste of time! He finds nothing there, nothing at all. In actual fact there are two boys in there, curled under a bush, but he doesn't see them. And he is stupid enough to think he was imagining things, or that perhaps it was only an animal in the undergrowth. He feels he's very good at what he does, and he's proved that now. And he is very pleased with himself as he returns to the car.

And here they come at last, his partners. The two spies crawling out from the undergrowth see them as well.

'Look, it's the professor,' whispers Kalle. 'They're kidnapping him too!'

Is it true? Or is it only a bad dream? Is that really the professor they are frogmarching towards the car? A wildly resisting, furious, desperate professor, with his hands tied behind his back and a gag over his mouth?

It is nightmarish and dreadful, but it isn't a dream. It's starting to get light now, and everything can be seen in awful clarity. The dust the professor's feet are kicking up as he struggles is not a dream. The car door slamming behind him is also horribly real. Now the car races down the hill and disappears. The road stands empty in the dawn light. It could have been a bad dream, all of it, if it wasn't for the faint smell of petrol in the air.

And if wasn't for a small, wet handkerchief lying on the roadside. Eva-Lotta's handkerchief.

The town is sleeping below, but it will wake up soon. The first rays of the sun are already glinting on the golden cockerel weathervane on the Town Hall.

'Holy moly,' said Kalle.

'Holy moly is right,' said Anders. 'What are you waiting for, Kalle? Are you Master Detective Blomkvist or aren't you?'

4

The road twists and turns as it makes its way through the green summer countryside. Past rocky hillsides, small glittering lakes and glades of fir trees, between white trunks of silver birch trees, meadows full of flowers, and fields of waving crops. Round many corners and down winding lanes, it finally makes its way to the coast and the sea.

A certain large black car is also making its way there on this beautiful summer morning, at breathtaking speed, screeching round corners and throwing up clouds of dust. It is a perfectly normal kind of car, but even so an observant onlooker might notice something unusual. It is, in fact, leaving an odd little trail behind it. Through a side window a girl's hand appears from time to time and after the car has passed, scraps of red paper, and sometimes small chunks of bun, are left behind on the gritty road. Yes, bun! Not for nothing is Eva-Lotta a baker's daughter, with an endless supply of buns in her pockets. The scraps of red paper are from a poster, torn down from a lamp post seconds before she slipped into the car where Rasmus was sleeping. 'Grand Summer Party' it says in large black letters on the poster. 'Tombola, Dancing, Tea Tent'. Thank goodness for Lillköping's Athletic Association and their poster, because it looks like it's going to be a long journey and how long will a couple of buns last? Soon Eva-Lotta will have to ration the buns as well as the scraps of paper. She must leave a piece of red paper behind at every road junction, otherwise how will her rescuers know which way to go? Will there even be any rescuers? And if not, how will this adventure end?

Eva-Lotta looks around inside the car and takes stock of the situation. The professor is sitting beside her on the back seat, still tied up, with a gag over his mouth and despair in his eyes. On his other side sits the man who so cleverly guarded the car. In the front seat is the man called Nick, with the sleeping Rasmus on his lap. Beside him at the wheel is the other wall-climber—Blom, his name is, so Eva-Lotta has learned. She takes it all in and then her gaze turns to look through the windscreen. They are racing through the beautiful Swedish summer landscape. The fields of ripe oats with their daisies and cornflowers are so typically Swedish. The white silver birch trees, too. Only this car and its strange passengers don't belong in the scene. They belong in an American gangster film. Eva-Lotta's heart beats faster when she thinks that the two goons in the front seat are in actual fact kidnappers.

Kidnappers! It seems crazy in such a sunny Swedish setting! Kidnappers ought to arrive in pouring rain on a dark autumn evening in Chicago!

Nick must have felt her gaze on the back of his neck, because he turns round and glares at her.

'Who in the blazes asked you to get mixed up in this?' he says. 'What made you get in the car, you stupid brat?'

Eva-Lotta is afraid, but more than that she is angry. And she doesn't intend letting that brute find out how desperately anxious she is.

'Don't worry about me,' she says. 'You'd be better off thinking about what you're going tell the police when they come looking for you!'

The professor's eyes look encouragingly at her and that makes her feel braver. She is grateful he is here, even if at the moment he is helpless. At least he is an adult, and on her side.

Nick grunts threateningly but turns away from her without saying any more. He has a thick neck and fair hair that could do with a trim, thinks Eva-Lotta. How else could she describe him? A description! If Kalle were here he would immediately start memorising a description. It's best she starts doing that, seeing as he isn't here, so that she will be able to assist the police. If she ever gets the chance to tell them!

That Nick has a pair of blue eyes that are stupid-looking but crafty at the same time, and an ugly, good-natured, red face. Yes, his face really is good-natured, even though he looks grumpy at the moment. Not the brightest bulb on the Christmas tree, thinks Eva-Lotta, and flatters herself by thinking her descriptions are way cleverer than Kalle's, who only talks about eye colour, birthmarks, and so on, but nothing about the person's character. So, what about the others? Blom is dark-haired, pale and spotty, and looks lazy. A bit careless, thinks Eva-Lotta, and he would probably do anything for money. And as for the one on the back seat, he's practically an imbecile. He looks a complete nothing with his sandy-coloured hair, hardly any chin and less intelligence than her little fingernail. What in all the world can have persuaded these three clowns to have a go at kidnapping? There must be some plan behind it, although none of the three looks like they could organize a bun fight in a bakery. But perhaps someone else is doing the organizing? Someone waiting in another place?

All of a sudden the car swerves onto a bumpy forest track. Quickly Eva-Lotta scatters a whole handful of crumbs and bits of paper out of the window, because the rescuers could easily lose the trail here. This looks like a private road, and certainly not one meant for traffic, judging from the way the car bounces and jolts over the rough surface. It jolts so much it wakes Rasmus up. First he half opens a pair of sleepy brown eyes, then he sits up with a start and stares at Nick.

'Are you the man who's come to mend our stove and . . . ?' He stops halfway through the sentence.

Eva-Lotta reaches out her hand and pats him on the cheek.

'I'm here, Rasmus,' she says. 'Aren't you glad I'm here? Your dad's here too, but . . .'

'Where are we going, Eeba-Lotta?' asks Rasmus.

Nick answers instead of Eva-Lotta.

'We're taking a little drive,' he says, with an amused little laugh. 'We're only taking a little drive.'

'Aren't you the man who's come to mend our kitchen stove?' Rasmus still wanted to know. 'Daddy, is he?'

But his dad doesn't answer.

Clearly Nick thinks this is a hilarious question. He laughs even louder.

'Mend your stove? No, little fella, not this time.'

It was as if the question had put him in a good mood. He sits Rasmus upright and suddenly begins to sing:

'There's a worm at the bottom of my garden
And his name is Wiggly Woo!'

'And what's your name?' asks Rasmus, interested.

'Nick,' says Nick, with a grin. *'And my name is Nicky Woo!'* he sings loudly.

'I think you should mend our stove,' says Rasmus. 'But it's just like Daddy says: "Promises, nothing but promises".'

Eva-Lotta looks at the professor in concern. He has other things to think about at the moment, apart from a kitchen stove that doesn't work. She pats his arm reassuringly, and he sends her a look of thanks.

Then, furtively, she drops her very last snippet of red paper out of the window. It drifts playfully in the sunlight before falling to the ground and staying there. Will anyone find it? And if so, when?

'No, no, we won't run and get the police,' said Kalle. 'There's no time now. We've got to follow those hoodlums and see which way they go.'

'Wonderful,' said Anders. 'Run and shout! That car doesn't stand a chance with a sprinter like you on its heels.'

Kalle didn't bother answering such a sarcastic remark. Instead, he charged through the front gate and up to the professor's motorbike.

'Come on!' he shouted. 'We'll take this!'

Anders looked at him with a mixture of fear and admiration.

'We can't . . .' he began, but Kalle interrupted him.

'We *must!*' he said. 'This is what you might call an emergency situation. You can't worry about stuff like driving licences when people's lives are at risk.'

'You drive much better than your dad, anyway,' said Anders.

They wheeled the motorbike onto the road. There

were a couple of faint tyre marks left in the sand by the car, but that was the only the clue the kidnappers had left. The black car was already far away. Which way had it gone?

'Eva-Lotta said she would do what Hansel and Gretel did,' shouted Kalle, as they sped down the hill. 'What did they do, remind me?'

'Scatter breadcrumbs behind them,' yelled Anders. 'And white pebbles.'

'Well, if Eva-Lotta's got any white pebbles with her in the car, she's more amazing than I thought,' said Kalle. 'But that would be just like her. She always thinks of something.'

They reached the first road junction, and Kalle braked. Which way? Which way?

There was a tiny piece of red paper caught in the grass on the verge. 'Dancing', it said. But there are always so many pieces of paper littering the roadsides, so they didn't pay much attention to it. A short distance away was something else. A piece of dough, broken off from a cinnamon bun by the look of things. Anders pointed at it and called out triumphantly. Eva-Lotta really was doing the same as Hansel and Gretel! And there was another scrap of red paper a couple of metres away. So the pieces of paper did mean something!

Feeling encouraged, they chose the road that led to the coast. They had forgotten their tiredness. You couldn't really say they were happy, but behind their worry was a strange kind of excitement. The engine purred under them and smoothly covered mile after mile of the snaking road that would lead them to an entirely unknown destination where unknown dangers waited. It was the blend of danger and speed that caused the peculiar excitement they felt.

They stared straight ahead. Here and there were the bits of red paper, left like jolly little greetings from Eva-Lotta.

Finally they came to the forest track. Came to it—and almost drove straight past. It was so insignificant you would scarcely notice it. But at the last minute Anders discovered a familiar red scrap waving, in among the fir trees.

'Stop!' he yelled. 'We're going the wrong way. They turned off into the woods.'

What a pretty little forest track it was! The morning sun filtered in between the trees, shining on the dark green moss and the pink Linnea flowers. A blackbird was sitting in the top of a pine tree, warbling happily, as if there was no evil in the world.

But as Kalle and Anders steered between the pines they felt all too strongly that the blackbird was wrong. With every fibre of their being they knew they would soon have to face a harmful and threatening situation which had nothing at all to do with flowers and birdsong.

The road began to slope, down and down. Something blue showed between the trees. The sea! And where the road came to an end was an old dilapidated wooden jetty sticking out into the water. At the far end of the jetty a final greeting from Eva-Lotta—her red hair slide.

They stood gazing thoughtfully across the water. The thin morning mist was beginning to lift and the sun dappled the surface of the water as it rippled gently in the dawn wind. How deathly quiet it was here! As quiet as the morning of creation, before there were any people in the world.

Tree-covered islands and tiny rocky skerries hid the horizon. You would almost think this narrow, blue bay was a lake. A few hundred metres beyond the jetty was a large island, blocking the way to the open sea. A huge, hilly, wooded island that looked entirely uninhabited.

But no, it wasn't uninhabited! Above the treetops a thin spiral of smoke rose up to the sky.

'So there's our den of thieves,' said Kalle.

'Let's get them,' said Anders.

'Do you think we can swim that far?'

'Of course we can,' said Anders. 'No problem. And seeing as there isn't a boat . . .'

There was a shack beside the jetty. Kalle walked over to it and felt the door. It was locked. Could there be a boat inside? There was a car, at least, he said to himself, as he looked at the tyre prints in the dewy grass outside. The black car would be hidden inside—he knew that all of a sudden, without a shadow of a doubt. And he felt immensely satisfied that they had managed to track down the kidnappers this far. They were right to have chased after them so quickly, he knew that now. The wind and the birds would soon have wiped out Eva-Lotta's trail, and then who would have thought to look in this remote and uninhabited part of the coast?

Kalle weighed up the distance to the island. Yes, they would have to swim there, but it was within their reach. But first they must hide the motorbike in the trees.

As they staggered ashore, blue with cold after their long swim, they felt like soldiers invading enemy territory. And invading enemy-held land stark naked was pretty horrible. Without clothes you felt even more helpless and vulnerable.

But there was no sign of the enemy, so they sat on a sunny rock to get dry and feel the warmth on their bodies. They untied their bundles of clothing and decided their shirts and jeans weren't too wet to be worn.

'I wonder what the Reds would say if they knew what we were doing?' said Kalle, with his head somewhere inside his shirt.

'"Typical Detective Blomkvist", that's what they'd say,'

Anders said confidently. 'You bump into thieves and bandits wherever you go.'

By now Kalle had his shirt on. He faced Anders, his head on one side, thinking. A pair of long brown legs stuck out from under his outgrown shirt and he looked very childlike and not at all like a master detective.

'Yes, it's rather strange really, the scrapes we get into over and over again,' he said.

'Yep,' agreed Anders. 'The stuff that happens to us usually only happens in books.'

'Maybe this is a book,' said Kalle.

'What? Have you gone doolally?' said Anders.

'Maybe we don't exist,' said Kalle, his thoughts miles away. 'We might only be a couple of boys in a book someone has made up.'

'You might be,' said Anders, annoyed. 'It wouldn't surprise me if you were a misprint, when it comes down to it. But not me, I can tell you that!'

'You don't know that,' Kalle insisted. 'You might only exist in a book I've made up.'

'Oh, man,' said Anders. 'In that case you are in a book that I've made up, and I'm starting to regret making you up already!'

'Well, whatever. I'm hungry,' said Kalle.

It was a waste of precious time doubting their own existence, they realized that. A more important and more dangerous mission lay ahead. Somewhere beyond those fir trees was a house with a chimney sending out a thin spiral of smoke. Somewhere there, were people. Somewhere there, was Eva-Lotta and Rasmus and the professor. It was absolutely crucial to find them.

'We'll go in that direction,' said Kalle, pointing towards the trees. 'Over there, where we saw the smoke.'

The path they followed ran between crowded pine trees, over mossy piles of rocks, across marshy land, through low blueberry bushes, past anthills and between tangles of wild roses. They kept perfectly quiet and alert, ready to flee if things became dangerous. And it felt as if things would become dangerous. When Kalle, who was leading, suddenly threw himself behind a pine tree, Anders turned pale with fright and shot like lightning after him, not bothering to waste time asking questions.

'There!' said Kalle, pointing between the trees. 'Look over there!'

It wasn't a frightening sight Anders saw, as he peered cautiously from behind a branch—quite the opposite.

A holiday cottage, a very expensive one by the look of it, sheltered from harsh winds by the thick forest around it, and with a sunny, sloping lawn in front. A beautiful lawn with velvety grass. And in the middle of the grass was the professor, with Rasmus on his lap. Yes, it was true, it really was them sitting there! Rasmus and the professor—and one other person.

'I don't think you are being very sensible, Professor Rasmusson,' said the other person. He was right—the professor wasn't being particularly sensible at this very moment. He looked ready to self-combust with fury. It was clear he wanted nothing more than to hurl himself at the man opposite him. He was only prevented by the fact that he had Rasmus on his lap and was still tied up.

'Quite incredibly foolish,' the man went on. 'I admit the way I've gone about things is a little unusual, but I had no choice. This matter is extremely important. I really had to have a talk with you.'

'Go to hell,' said the professor. 'Either you've been reading too many crime novels, or you've lost your mind.'

The other man gave a dry, superior little laugh and began pacing backwards and forwards over the grass. He was a tall, stocky man in his forties, with a face that would have been handsome if it hadn't been so alarmingly hard.

'Don't concern yourself about the state of my mind,'

he said. 'The only thing I want to know is if you will accept my proposal.'

'And the only thing I want to know is when and how I can punch your lights out,' said the professor.

'I think he should do that right away,' whispered Kalle, behind the pine tree. Anders nodded in agreement.

But the stranger looked at the professor as if he was a foolish child.

'Why throw away a hundred thousand like that?' he said. 'I'm offering you a hundred thousand for the formula—that's a very good price, don't you agree? You don't even have to hand the documents over to me personally, if your conscience won't allow it. Just give me a small hint as to where I can find them.'

'Listen here, Professor Peters, or what the blazes your name is. Don't you understand the formula belongs to the Swedish government?'

Peters shrugged impatiently.

'Nobody needs to know it's your formula that's leaving the country. They can make super lightweight metals in other countries, you know. It's only a question of time. The reason I want to buy the formula from you is to save time.'

'Go and jump in the lake,' the professor said.

Peters' eyes narrowed.

'I *want* it,' he said. 'I want your formula. And I will get it.'

Up to now Rasmus had been sitting silently, but now he joined in the conversation.

'"I want, I want". That's not what you say. You have to say "Please".'

'Quiet, Rasmus,' said the professor, and hugged his son tightly.

Peters studied the two of them.

'That's a nice boy you've got there,' he said, threateningly. 'I'm sure you don't want to lose him.'

The professor said nothing, but he stared in disgust at the man facing him.

'Let's do a little trade-off,' Peters went on. 'You tell me where the documents are so that I can send a man to get them. You stay here until I'm sure they are they are the right documents, and then not only do you go free but you'll be a hundred thousand richer.'

'Put a sock in it,' said the professor. 'I can't bear hearing any more.'

'As I was saying, a hundred thousand richer,' Peters went on, as if he hadn't heard. In your own interest I advise you to go along with my proposal. Because if you don't . . .'

There was a brief, menacing silence.

'If I don't?' the professor sneered. 'What happens then?'

The shadow of a cruel little smile flickered over Peters' face.

'Then you've seen your son for the last time,' he said.

'You're even crazier than I thought,' said the professor. 'Do you really imagine I would allow myself to be scared by such an absurd threat?'

'We'll soon find out. It would be better if you could get it into your head that we mean business.'

'And it would be better if you could get it into your head that I will never reveal where I keep my documents.'

Rasmus sat bolt upright on his dad's lap and glared at Peters.

'No, and I'm not going to tell you either!' he said triumphantly. 'Even though I know where they are.'

The professor flinched.

'What kind of nonsense is that?' he said. 'Of course you don't.'

'Don't I?' said Rasmus. 'Do you want to bet?'

'Be quiet,' said the professor sharply. 'You've no idea what we're talking about.'

'Yes I have,' said Rasmus, unhappy that his dad doubted his ability to understand the conversation. 'You're talking about those pieces of paper with all the little red numbers on. The ones you said were very, *very* secret . . .'

'Yes, they're the ones we're talking about,' said Peters. 'But surely you don't know where they are, a little boy like you?'

The professor broke in angrily.

'This is getting us nowhere. Don't you understand that every single document is locked in a safety deposit box in a bank?'

Rasmus stared at his dad in dismay.

'Now you're lying, Daddy,' he said. 'Of course they're not in one of those . . . deposit box things.'

'Quiet, Rasmus!' roared the professor, with unusual severity.

But Rasmus believed this had to be sorted out. His daddy seemed to have forgotten the proper way to behave.

'They're not in a bank, I know they're not,' he insisted. 'Because I crept up behind you the other evening, Daddy, when you thought I was asleep. I stood on the stairs in the hall and watched you put . . .'

'Shut UP, Rasmus!' roared his father again, even louder than before.

'Why are you yelling at me?' Rasmus asked indignantly. 'I won't tell him where they are . . .'

Then he looked at Peters sympathetically.

'But I can tell you if you're getting hot or cold, like you do in hide and seek,' he said helpfully.

The professor shook him roughly.

'Will you be *quiet*!' he shouted.

'All right, all right, I will,' said Rasmus impatiently. 'I haven't told him anything, have I?'

He pouted and thought for a while.

'But you're nowhere near warm yet,' he said.

7

Eva-Lotta looked around her prison. Her very nice prison, to tell the truth. If only that Nick person hadn't hammered a couple of planks of wood across the window, she could have convinced herself that she was a welcome holiday guest on this island. Hadn't she been given a tiny guest cabin of her very own? Cosy, with green-checked bed linen on the four bunks along one wall, a screen hiding a table with a jug and bowl for washing, and by the window, a small table with books and magazines to help the guests pass the time. Of all the hostage hideaways in the world, this must be the strangest, thought Eva-Lotta.

There can't have been that many hostage hideaways with such a view, either. The window was open behind the wooden bars and it looked out on to a spectacularly beautiful summer landscape. The blue water, sparkling in the sunshine, wrapped itself around tiny green islands. Eva-Lotta took a deep breath. If only she could run down to the jetty along the narrow track covered in pine needles, and dive head first into the clear water, or stretch out on the jetty in the sun, shut her eyes and listen to the gentle lapping of the waves as the boats tugged at their moorings!

Yes, boats! The kidnappers' boats. They had several. Eva-Lotta could see the motor boat that had brought them here across the bay, and the three rowing boats bobbing next to it. And pulled up on the long wooden jetty was a large Canadian canoe.

This island was a distinctly comfortable place for kidnappers, thought Eva-Lotta. And with room for a whole army of them, if necessary. They hardly had to feel overcrowded. There were a few other little cabins dotted here and there at a suitable distance from the big house where the boss of the kidnapping outfit stayed. Maybe there was a kidnapper in every little cabin, each one in their own little den? If you banged on the door perhaps an angry little kidnapper would jump out and scare you half to death!

At this thought Eva-Lotta tossed her head and looked very determined. She wasn't going to let herself be scared half to death. How dare anyone treat Eva-Lotta Lisander like this! She would teach that Nick a lesson or two.

With clenched fists, she hammered and hammered on the door.

'Nick! Nick!' she shouted. 'Come and bring me some food! Otherwise I'll wreck the cabin!'

Anders and Kalle, who were lying beneath the pine tree, listening to the conversation between Peters and the professor, heard the racket and grinned. Thank goodness! Eva-Lotta was alive and well and clearly not at all crushed by her experience.

Nick also heard the racket, but he wasn't quite so thrilled about it. Muttering angrily to himself, he went to put a stop to it.

Eva-Lotta went quiet when she heard the key in the door. Nick stepped in, ready to give her what for, but he wasn't as quick thinking as Eva-Lotta, and she beat him to it.

'I don't think much of the service in this hotel,' she said.

Nick immediately forgot what it was he was going to say. He glared at Eva-Lotta, astonished and quite hurt.

'Now you listen to me,' he said. 'You just listen to me . . .'

'No, you listen to me,' said Eva-Lotta. 'The service at this hotel is rubbish. I want some food! Food, do you understand?'

'What have we done to deserve you?' said Nick. 'And it's all that blasted Svanberg's fault. He couldn't keep an eye on the car properly. It's going to be *very* entertaining to hear what the boss thinks of this.'

'Oh, you should be glad I'm here to entertain you,' said Eva-Lotta. 'It must be wonderful for a kidnapper to snatch two kids, when they only reckoned with one.'

'Now you listen to me,' said Nick. 'I don't like that kind of talk. I'm not your kidnapper.'

'Aren't you? Actually, that's precisely what you are, Kidnapper Nick. If you snatch a child, that makes you a kidnapper, didn't you know that?'

Once again Nick looked astonished and hurt. Clearly he hadn't looked at it from that angle before, and he certainly didn't like doing it now.

'I'm not your kidnapper,' he said, uncertainly. 'And anyway, you shouldn't be making so much noise,' he shouted, furious all of a sudden. He grabbed Eva-Lotta by the arms and shook her. 'Do you hear me? Stop making such a din, otherwise you'll regret it.'

Eva-Lotta looked him steadily in the eye. For some reason she had a vague idea that's what you did when you wanted to tame a wild animal.

'I want some food,' she said. 'And I'll make as much noise as a whole classful of kids if I don't get any.'

Nick swore and let her go. He walked towards the door.

'All right, all right, you'll get some food,' he said. 'Is there anything in particular Her Majesty would like?'

'Um, bacon and eggs would be nice,' said Eva-Lotta. 'I always like that for breakfast. Eggs fried on both sides, please. And get a move on, if you wouldn't mind.'

Nick slammed the door behind him. Eva-Lotta heard the key turn in the lock, and she heard Nick swear outside.

But shortly afterwards she heard something else, something that filled her with indescribable joy. She heard the White Roses' signal outside, under the window. Incredibly faint, but still—it was the White Roses' signal. More beautiful than all the angels' harps in heaven!

8

Kalle woke up with a start. He looked around him, confused. Where was he? Was it evening or morning? And why was Anders lying there fast asleep with his hair flopped over his face?

Gradually his brain cleared. He was in the den he and Anders had built, and it was evening. The sun was setting, and outside the last rays were painting the trunks of the pines red. And Anders—well, he was fast asleep from exhaustion, naturally! What a day! Strictly speaking, it had begun yesterday evening, at the castle ruins. And now it was evening again. He and Anders had slept almost all afternoon, and they certainly needed it. But first they had built this fantastic den. Kalle reached out and felt the wall made from fir tree branches. Oh, how he loved this den! It was their home, a little refuge they had made as far away from the kidnappers as they could possibly get. No one would find them here. The den was nestled in a dip between two small ridges. No one would ever discover it unless they happened to stumble over it by chance. It was out of the wind, too, and they had soft branches to sleep on. The rocks on either side still held some of the day's warmth, so they wouldn't be cold in the night. Oh, what a terrific den it was!

'Are you hungry?' said Anders. It was so unexpected that Kalle jumped.

'Oh, you're awake, then?'

Anders sat up on his bed of soft branches. They had left a pattern on his cheek.

'I'm so hungry I could almost eat boiled fish,' he said.

'Don't talk about it,' said Kalle. 'I'm going to start eating tree bark any minute.'

'Yes, well, when you've lived on nothing but blue-berries all day, you need something solid to chew on,' said Anders.

Eva-Lotta was their only hope. She had promised to get them something to eat.

'I'll torment the life out of Nick,' she had promised them. 'I'll tell him the doctor told me to eat every two hours. You'll get some food, don't worry! Come back when it's dark!'

That had been in the morning. They had stood under her window, whispering through the wooden slats which barred her escape, ready to run at the first sign of danger. As soon as Nick had arrived with her food, they had rushed off like a couple of scared lizards, even though the smell of the bacon he had brought was like nectar to their noses. They only had time to catch Eva-Lotta's first caustic remark to Nick:

'Do you think I've come here to go on a diet?'

They didn't hang around to hear Nick's reply. By that time they were well into the woods.

Gradually they had made their way over to the far side of the island. And that's where they had been all day, building their den, swimming from the rocks on the shore, sleeping—and eating blueberries. And now they were about as starving hungry as anyone could be.

'All we have to do is wait until it gets dark,' moaned Anders.

They crawled out of their den and climbed up onto the rocks. They found a comfy little crevice to sit in and wait for nightfall and the darkness that would save them from starvation. They sat there, miserably watching the most stunning sunset they had ever seen in their lives, but the only thing they felt was frustration because it was going so slowly. The sky burned like an inferno above the treetops on the mainland. A small slice of sun was still visible, but soon that would vanish into the dark shadows over there. Darkness, that wonderful, blessed darkness, would fall over land and sea and over everyone who needed protecting from kidnappers. If only it would go faster!

The rocks they were sitting on dropped steeply to the water, and they could hear the ripple of waves breaking gently over the pebbles below. Somewhere across the water a sea bird cried, and it was a melancholy sound. Apart from that, all was quiet.

'This is starting to get on my nerves,' said Kalle.

'And I'm wondering what they're thinking back home,' said Anders. 'Do you reckon they've put out a search for us on the radio yet?'

As soon as Anders said that, they remembered the note Eva-Lotta had left on her pillow the evening before: *'Now don't make a big fuss! I've just gone out to fight a battle and I'll be home soon, I think, ha ha ha.'* Even if her parents were pretty annoyed by now, and maybe even a little worried about her disappearance, it wasn't likely they would have contacted the police straight away after reading a note like that. And after Anders' and Kalle's parents had discussed it with the baker and his wife, their minds would probably be put at rest too, along with some mutterings about the stupid stunts the White Roses got up to. And perhaps that was just as well. Who knew if it was a wise move, getting the police involved? Kalle had read enough kidnapping stories to know how dangerous that could be. In any case, first of all they had to ask the advice of the professor. If they could only to speak to him.

A light was shining in Peters' house, but apart from that there was darkness everywhere. And silence. It was a silence so deep you could almost hear it. If there were any living people here at all, they must all be asleep.

Wrong! They were not all asleep. Horribly wide awake, the professor lay on his bunk, torturing himself with endless brooding. For all of his thirty-five years he had been used to finding a solution to whatever problem came his way. But his present situation was so incredibly preposterous that all he could do was shake his head. Quite simply, there was nothing he could do. He was forced to admit that to himself, in a powerless, frustrating rage. There was nothing he could do but wait. And what was he waiting for? For someone to miss him, and start looking? But he had rented that old house in Lillköping so that he could be left in peace. He had planned to live there on his own with Rasmus all through the summer. It might be a long time before anyone even noticed he was missing. Having thought that far, the professor leapt out of his bunk. There was no chance of getting any sleep. Oh, he would like to rip that Peters to shreds!

Eva-Lotta couldn't sleep either. She was sitting by the window, listening intently for any sound outside. Was that the night wind rustling in the trees, or had Anders and Kalle finally returned?

The day had been long, so terribly long. For someone who loved her freedom it was unbearable to be shut in for a whole day. With a shudder Eva-Lotta thought of all those poor people wasting away in captivity. She wanted to go round the world opening every prison door and releasing every single one of the world's prisoners from their dungeons! Because this was the worst thing of all—not being able to get out when you wanted to. Something dangerously close to panic came over her as she sat there, and she threw herself wildly at the barred window that separated her from freedom. But then she remembered Rasmus and realized she had to control herself. She didn't want to wake Rasmus. He was sleeping soundly in one of the bunks. She could hear his regular breathing in the darkness and her panic subsided. At least she wasn't alone.

Then, breaking through the silence, came the long-awaited signal. The signal of the White Roses, and immediately afterwards an urgent whisper:

'Eva-Lotta, have you got any food for us?'

'I should say so,' said Eva-Lotta.

As fast as she could she slung sandwiches, slices of ham, boiled potatoes and cold, greasy sausages out between the bars. She didn't get as much as a thank you from the boys outside, because all they could get out between bites was a grunt or two. Now it was within reach, their hunger seemed worse than ever, and they crammed all the delicious food into their mouths almost without chewing.

Eventually they had to pause for breath, and Kalle mumbled:

'I'd forgotten how good food can be.'

Eva-Lotta smiled in the darkness, as happy as a mother giving her hungry children bread. She whispered earnestly:

'Are you full up yet?'

'I think I am, actually,' said Anders, in surprise. 'That was the best—'

Kalle interrupted him.

'Listen Eva-Lotta, do you know where the professor is?'

'He's locked in the little cabin near that rocky cliff,' said Eva-Lotta. 'The one closest to the water.'

'Is Rasmus there too, do you think?'

'No, Rasmus is with me. He's asleep.'

'Yes, I'm asleep,' said a tiny voice in the darkness.

'Oh, you're awake,' said Eva-Lotta.

'Yes, I am. You can't help waking up when people are chomping and gobbling.' He padded over to Eva-Lotta and climbed onto her lap.

'Have Kalle and Anders come?' he asked, happily. 'Are you going to fight battles? Can't I be a White Rose too?'

'That depends if you can keep quiet,' said Kalle in a low voice. 'We might let you be a White Rose if you promise not to say you've seen me and Anders.'

'All right then!' said Rasmus.

'Not a squeak to Nick or anyone else that we've been here, understand?'

'Why? Doesn't Nick like you?'

'Nick doesn't know we're here,' said Anders. 'And he

mustn't find out, either. Nick is a kidnapper, you see.'

'Aren't kidnappers nice?' asked Rasmus.

'No, not much,' said Eva-Lotta.

'Well, I think they're nice,' said Rasmus. 'I think Nick is ever so nice. Why mustn't kidnappers know secrets?'

'Because they mustn't,' said Kalle. 'And you'll never be allowed to be a White Rose if you can't keep quiet.'

'But I can!' shouted Rasmus, eagerly. He was prepared to keep quiet until the end of his days, if only he could be a White Rose.

At that moment Eva-Lotta heard heavy footsteps outside, and her heart did a somersault of fear.

'Disappear!' she whispered. 'Hurry! Nick's coming.'

The next second the key turned in the lock. The beam from a torch lit the room, and Nick asked suspiciously:

'Who are you talking to?'

'I'll give you three guesses,' said Eva-Lotta. 'In here are Rasmus and me, and me and Rasmus. I don't normally talk to myself, so who do you think I was talking to?'

'But you're a kidnapper and kidnappers mustn't ever find out secrets,' said Rasmus, kindly.

'Now just you listen to me,' said Nick, and he took a threatening step towards Rasmus. 'Is it your turn now to start accusing me of being a kidnapper?'

Rasmus grasped his large hand and looked trustingly up at the furious face looming over him.

'But I think kidnappers are nice,' he went on. 'I think

you're nice, Uncle Nick!'

Nick muttered something inaudible and turned to leave.

'Am I supposed to starve to death in this place?' said Eva-Lotta. 'Why haven't I had any supper?'

Nick turned round and looked at her in genuine astonishment.

'Your poor parents,' he said. 'They must have a job keeping you fed.'

Eva-Lotta smiled.

'I've certainly got a healthy appetite,' she said, cheerfully.

But all Nick did was lift Rasmus from her lap and sit him on his bunk.

'I think you should get some sleep now, young'un,' he said.

'But I'm not sleepy,' complained Rasmus. 'I've been asleep all day.'

Nick tucked him into his bed without a word.

'Could you cover my feet?' asked Rasmus. 'I don't like it when my toes stick out.'

Chuckling, and looking rather confused, Nick did as he was asked. Then he stood looking down at Rasmus thoughtfully.

'You're a funny little fish,' he said.

The boy's dark hair rested on his pillow. In the dim light he looked unnaturally angelic as he lay there.

'Oh, you're so nice, Uncle Nick,' he said. 'Come here and I'll give you a cuddle. One of those big squeezy ones I give Daddy.'

Before Nick had time to think, Rasmus wrapped his arms around his neck and hugged him as hard as his five-year-old arms could manage.

'Does it hurt?' he asked, hopefully.

Nick was quiet at first, but then he mumbled:

'No, it doesn't hurt. It doesn't hurt at all.'

High up on top of the rocks stood the small cabin where Peters was holding his famous guest. It was like an eagles' nest, and it could be reached from only one direction. The back of the cabin overlooked the cliff that dropped almost vertically to the beach below.

'We've got to climb up there,' said Kalle, pointing with a greasy finger at the professor's window.

After their adventure in the castle ruins, Anders wasn't all that keen on climbing anything steep, even if this wasn't quite as terrifyingly high.

'Can't we sneak in the proper way at the front, like normal people?' he suggested.

'And walk straight into the arms of Nick or someone else?' said Kalle. 'Not likely!'

'You climb,' said Anders. 'I'll stay down here and keep watch.'

Kalle didn't think twice. He licked the remaining sausage grease from his fingers and set off.

It wasn't quite so dark now. The flat disc of the moon

rose steadily above the trees. Kalle didn't know whether to be grateful for that or not. It was easier to climb when there was moonlight, but that also made it easier for the person doing the climbing to be discovered. Perhaps it was best to be grateful for the light of the moon, but also grateful that it disappeared behind clouds from time to time.

Kalle held his breath and climbed. The climb itself wasn't especially difficult, but the thought that he could have a pack of kidnappers on his tail at any moment made him break out in a cold sweat.

Carefully he felt for hand and footholds and worked his way slowly upwards. At times it felt practically impossible. For a few dizzying moments it felt as if he was reaching out into empty space, and he found it hard to get a grip. But it was as if his feet instinctively found their way among the crevices and roots, and he always found something to cling onto.

Only once the instinct left his big toe, and he kicked a stone loose. With a massive crash it hurtled down the rock face. Kalle almost plummeted after it in terror—it was a close thing. But at the last minute he was saved by a tree root that he managed to grab. He clung on to it nervously and for a long time didn't dare move.

Anders heard the din as the stone came crashing down. He sprang to one side so it wouldn't hit him on the head, and muttered angrily to himself:

'He might as well blow a trumpet as well, to let them know he's on his way.'

Evidently Anders was the only one who had heard the noise. And when Kalle, his heart hammering, had waited for a minute and nothing happened, he let go of the tree root and continued climbing.

Inside his dark room, the professor paced up and down like a caged animal. This was unbearable, absolutely unbearable! It was enough to drive you insane. It was highly likely he would go insane, just like that madman Peters clearly was. He was left to the mercy of a mentally deranged person. He didn't know what they had done with Rasmus. He didn't know if he would ever get out of here. And it was a dark as the grave. Damn that Peters— he could at least have given him a candle! Just wait till he got his hands on that villain . . . but wait, what was that? The professor stopped dead in his tracks. Was it only a figment of his overactive imagination, or was there really someone knocking at his window? But that confounded window he had spent the entire confounded day staring out of—it directly overlooked a vertical drop . . . No one could possibly . . . Good heavens, there it was again, the knocking! There really was someone there. Beside himself with hope and despair he rushed over to the window and opened it. No prison window could be more effectively barred than this one, but it was done in such a clever way that from the outside it looked like a perfectly nice, ordinary fishing cabin. Despite the iron bars at the back.

'Is there anyone there?' whispered the professor. 'Who's there?'

'It's only me, Kalle Blomkvist.'

It sounded like ghostly murmuring but it was enough to make the professor shake with excitement. His hands gripped the iron bars eagerly.

'Kalle Blomkvist? Who . . . ? Oh, I remember now. Please, Kalle, do you know anything about Rasmus?'

'He's over in Eva-Lotta's cabin. He's okay!'

'Thank God! Thank God for that!' The professor sighed in relief. 'Peters told me I'd seen him for the last time.'

'Shall we try and get hold of the police?' Kalle asked urgently.

The professor held his head in his hands.

'No, not the police. At least, not yet. Oh, I don't know what to think! I'm beginning to believe Peters means what he says. If it wasn't for Rasmus . . . No, no, I daren't involve the police. Not until Rasmus is safe!'

He gripped the bars again and whispered:

'The worst thing is, Rasmus knows where I keep the copies of my discovery. And Peters knows that he knows. It won't be long before he has made Rasmus tell him.'

'Where are they? Can we go and get them, me and Anders?'

'Do you really think you can?' The professor was so

eager, his voice cracked. 'Good grief, if only you could. I've hidden them behind . . .'

But some ghastly fate had decided that Kalle would never find out that precious secret, because at that instant the door was unlocked and the professor fell as silent as if he had been hit by lightning. He forced himself to keep quiet, even though he could have cried out with rage and disappointment. Only one more second and he would have had time to say what he wanted to say! But here was Peters, in the doorway. He was holding a small oil lamp, and he greeted his hostage politely.

'Good evening, Professor Rasmusson!'

The professor did not answer.

'That damned Nick, hasn't he given you a lamp?' he went on. 'Well, here you are, have this!'

He put the lamp on the table and smiled. Still the professor said nothing.

'I can say hello from Rasmus,' Peters said. 'It looks like I'm going to have to send him far, far away.'

The professor made a move as if to throw himself over his tormentor, but Peters held up a hand to warn him off.

'Nick and Blom are outside,' he said. 'If you want a fight, we'll fight back. And we have Rasmus—don't forget that.'

The professor sank down on the bed and buried his face in his hands. They had Rasmus! They held all the cards! And all he had was Kalle Blomkvist. Kalle was his only hope—and he must control himself, he must!

Peters strolled round the room and stopped with his back to the window.

'Well, goodnight, my friend,' he said calmly. 'You can think about it for a while. But not for too long, I'm afraid.'

Outside, Kalle stood pressed against the wall. He heard Peters' voice as close as if the man had been speaking directly to him. Terrified, he took a step backwards. But his foot found only a treacherous tuft of grass, and with an ear-splitting crash the master detective plunged down the steep rock face and landed at Anders' feet rather quicker than he had planned.

Kalle groaned, and Anders leaned over him in alarm.

'Are you hurt? Do you feel all right?'

'Oh yes, I feel absolutely marvellous,' said Kalle, and groaned again. But he had no time to think about his bruises, because from the cabin above he heard Peters yell:

'Nick! Blom! Where are you? Search down below! Use the searchlights! Move it!'

'Holy macaroni,' whispered Anders.

'Precisely,' said Kalle. 'We're in trouble now.'

Before they even had time to think about running, the searchlights began flashing through the trees. Any minute now they could be caught in a beam—what a horrendous thought! Nick and Blom came charging towards them—the boys could hear them getting closer. They wanted to run but fear rooted them to the spot. When Nick was no more than five or ten paces away they squeezed themselves, in panic, into a crack between two rocks. It was the most useless, pathetic little crack, but they squashed themselves in as if they were trying to burst it open. This must be what it feels like to be a hunted animal when the bloodhounds are closing in, thought Kalle, in despair.

Sure enough, the bloodhounds were right on top of them! The beam from the search lights flickered from side to side. Kalle and Anders clung together and suddenly began to think of their mothers at home. The moon shone treacherously through the trees—as if the searchlights weren't bad enough!

'This way, Nick,' called Blom, and his voice sounded horribly close. 'Let's check in that clump of trees over there. If there's anyone here, then he's there.'

'He can't be both here and there,' grinned Nick. 'Anyway, I think the boss is imagining things.'

'We'll soon find out,' said Blom grimly.

Mum, Mum, Mum, thought Kalle. *They're coming. We're snookered. Goodbye forever.*

They were right on top of them, and for a split second the beam from Nick's searchlight shone directly into the crack in the rock. But sometimes miracles happen.

'What the . . . ? Something's wrong with my

searchlight,' said Nick.

Oh thank you, thank you, thank you! Nick's searchlight had gone out. And to make the miracle even more perfect, at the very same time, the moon disappeared behind a large cloud. Blom crept in between the trees, with Nick hot on his heels. He was fiddling with his searchlight.

'If there's anyone here, then he's there,' he muttered, imitating Blom. 'There you are, it's come on again!' he went on happily, aiming the beam among the tree trunks. But there was no one there, and Nick nudged Blom and said: 'I told you the boss was imagining things. It's his nerves. There's not a single blighter here.'

'No, it's as empty as my wallet,' grumbled Blom. 'But we'll go on a bit further, just to make sure.'

Yes, you do that, just to make sure! thought Kalle. And as if on cue he and Anders bolted the few metres to the trees, and crept in under the ones packed tightly together. Their experience with the White Roses had taught them that there was no safer place than the one that had just been searched.

Nick and Blom were soon back. They passed so close to the trees that Kalle could have reached out a hand and touched them They also passed the narrow crack in the rock, and Blom shone his light into it extremely thoroughly. But there was no one there.

'If there's anyone here, then he isn't there anyway,' said Nick, and he also aimed his light into the crack.

'No, he most certainly isn't,' whispered Kalle, breathing a sigh of relief.

10

A new day dawned, and the sun still shone down on the good and the bad. It woke Kalle and Anders as they slept peacefully on the soft branches in their den.

'Well, what shall we have for breakfast today?' Anders asked.

'For breakfast, blueberries,' said Kalle. 'Then for lunch, blueberries. And for dinner, just for a change, we could have . . . more blueberries.'

'Oh no, Eva-Lotta is providing dinner,' said Anders emphatically.

They remembered the day before and sighed longingly at thought of everything they had gobbled up. But they also remembered the awful experience afterwards, and they shuddered. They knew they would have to do it all again this evening. It was unavoidable. The professor was waiting for them, they knew that. Someone had to climb up to his window again to find out where the copies were hidden. If they could rescue the professor's documents then at least they would have done one good deed in their lifetime. Kalle felt the grazes on his arms and legs.

'I might as well do it again. A few more bruises won't make any difference,' he said. 'But for now, some breakfast would be nice.'

'I'm in charge of breakfast,' said Anders. 'Stay where you are. You can have blueberries in bed.'

Rasmus and Eva-Lotta also had breakfast in bed, but a considerably more substantial one than Anders and Kalle. Obviously Nick had decided to silence the mouth of the hoity-toity girl by stuffing it full of food. He had loaded the tray with ham and eggs, porridge and bread and cheese, enough for a whole regiment. He put it down in front of Eva-Lotta, who had just woken up.

'Come on, girl, up you get and eat, so you don't starve to death,' he said.

Eva-Lotta squinted sleepily at the tray.

'That's more like it,' she said approvingly. 'But perhaps tomorrow you could make us some waffles as well. That's if the police haven't nabbed you by then.'

Rasmus sat up quickly in his bed.

'The police mustn't nab Nick,' he said, his voice trembling. 'They can't nab people who are nice.'

'No, but they nab kidnappers,' said Eva-Lotta calmly, spreading a slice of bread with a thick layer of butter.

'Now you listen to me,' said Nick. 'I'm fed up with you going on and on about kidnappers!'

'And I'm fed up with being kidnapped!' said Eva-Lotta. 'So that makes it quits.'

Nick glared at her angrily.

'No one asked you to come. It would be a happy summer holiday here without you.'

He walked over to Rasmus and sat on the edge of his bed. Rasmus lifted a warm little hand and patted him on the cheek.

'I think kidnappers are nice,' he said. 'What shall we do today, Nick?'

'First you're going to get some breakfast down you,' said Nick. 'Then we'll see!'

Rasmus' opinion of Nick as a nice person stemmed from the first few hours he had spent on the island.

At the beginning Rasmus thought this stay on the island was an exciting adventure dreamed up by his dad. It was fun travelling in the car, fun going on the speedboat, the jetty here on this island was brilliant, and there were lots of boats. He was going to ask his dad if he could go swimming. But then that horrible man had come and spoiled everything. He talked to his dad in such a strange way, and then Daddy got angry and shouted at Rasmus, and then Daddy disappeared and Rasmus wasn't allowed to see him any more.

That's when he began to think the adventure wasn't

quite so much fun after all. He tried to hold back his tears, but the first muffled sobs turned quickly into floods of tears. Peters had pushed him roughly towards Nick and said: 'Take care of the brat!'

Nick scratched his head. It wasn't an easy job. He had no idea how to deal with a crying child, but he was prepared to do whatever it took to put an end to the awful racket.

'Why don't I make you a bow and some arrows?' he suggested, in desperation.

It worked like magic. Rasmus stopped crying as abruptly as he had started, and his belief in human kindness was restored.

They played with the bow and arrows for over two hours, and Rasmus was convinced—Nick was nice. And if what Eva-Lotta said was true, that Nick was a kidnapper, then kidnappers were nice.

The sun rose higher and higher in the sky and continued to shine down on the good and the not quite so good. It warmed the smooth rocks by the water, where Anders and Kalle passed the time. It shone down on Nick who sat on Eva-Lotta's porch carving bark boats, and on Rasmus who tested the finished boats in the water barrel. It shone on Eva-Lotta's blonde hair where she sat on her bunk bed and hated Nick because he wouldn't let her out. And it irritated Peters simply because on this beautiful summer day absolutely everything irritated him, and that included the sunshine. But despite Peters' irritation, the sun continued its journey steadily across the sky and eventually sank in the west and disappeared behind the trees on the mainland. And that brought the second day on the island to an end.

No, not the end. Now was only the beginning. It started with Peters walking into Eva-Lotta's cabin. He ignored Eva-Lotta—she wasn't the one he was interested in. Unfortunately enough she had happened to see Rasmus being snatched, and she had managed to slip into the car because that dunderhead Svanberg hadn't been keeping watch properly. It wasn't easy having her here, but that couldn't be helped, and she could prove useful by keeping the boy happy until his pig-headed father saw sense—that was all there was to say about Eva-Lotta. He needn't worry about her. Rasmus was the one he wanted to talk to.

Rasmus was already in bed, with five small bark boats on his blanket. His bow and arrows were hanging on the wall. He felt very content. This was a brilliant island, and kidnappers were nice.

'Listen to me, my lad,' said Peters, sitting down on the edge of the bed. 'What would you say if we had to keep you here all summer?'

A broad grin spread over Rasmus's face.

'All summer! Oh, you're so kind! Then me and Daddy can have our summer holiday here with you.'

One-nil to Rasmus, thought Eva-Lotta, and smiled.

But she made sure not to say anything. Peters wasn't the kind of person you said things to.

Nick was sitting on a chair by the window, looking pleased with himself, that much was obvious. At last, that insolent girl had been made to shut up!

Peters wasn't quite so pleased.

'Listen here, Rasmus . . .' he began, but Rasmus interrupted him, beaming with happiness.

'We can go swimming every day, can't we? I can swim five metres. Do you want to see me swim five metres?'

'All right,' said Peters. 'But . . .'

'It's going to be so much fun,' said Rasmus. 'Do you know what? One day last summer Marianne went under the water when we were swimming. Blub, blub, blub, she went. But then up she came again. Marianne can't swim as far as me.'

Peters gave a nervous little shriek.

'I couldn't care less how far you can swim. I want to know where your dad has hidden those documents with the red numbers on.'

Rasmus screwed up his eyes and looked at Peters with dislike.

'Bleeping bellybuttons, Peters, you're so horrible. Didn't you hear my daddy say I wasn't to tell you?'

'We don't care what your dad says right now. And by the way, a snivelling little kid like you should be polite to his elders. It's *Mr* Peters to you.'

'So that's what you're called,' said Rasmus, patting his very finest boat lovingly.

Peters gulped. He realized he would have to control himself if he was going to get anywhere.

'Rasmus, you can have something really special if you tell me,' he said kindly. 'I'll give you a steam engine.'

'I've already got a steam engine,' said Rasmus. 'Bark boats are much better.'

He held his very finest bark boat under Peters' nose.

'Have you ever seen a bark boat as nice as this one, Mr Peters?'

He pushed it from side to side over the blanket. It sailed across the ocean to America, where the cowboys were.

'When I grow up I'm going to be a cowboy and shoot people,' he said. 'But not women and children. I won't shoot them.'

Peters did not reply to this sensational piece of information. He forced himself to stay calm, and he tried to work out a way to get Rasmus to agree to what he asked.

The bark boat glided over the blanket, steered by a suntanned and rather grubby little hand.

'You're a kidnapper,' said Rasmus, keeping his eyes on the path his boat was taking over the ocean, and still with his mind on other things. 'You are a kidnapper,' he said. 'That's why you mustn't know any secrets.

Otherwise I'd tell you that Daddy's got them in a pile behind the bookshelf, but I won't . . . Oops, now I've told you anyway,' he said, surprised at himself.

'Oh, Rasmus,' groaned Eva-Lotta.

Peters leapt up.

'Did you hear that, Nick!' he said, and gave a hearty laugh. 'Did you hear? Oh, it's too good to be true. "Behind the bookcase". We'll get them tonight. Be ready to leave in one hour.'

'Okay, boss,' said Nick.

Peters hurried to the door, totally ignoring Rasmus' cries of anguish behind him.

'No-o! Come back! It doesn't count when you don't mean to say something. Come back, I said!'

11

The White Roses had all sorts of secret signals and warning signs. There were no less than three signs that meant 'Danger': there was the quick pull of the left earlobe, used in front of both comrades and enemies when they wanted to warn their comrades to watch out, the owl sound that summoned every White Rose milling about in the area to lend a hand fast, and lastly the major catastrophe howl that could only be used when deadly danger threatened and you were in dire distress.

Right now Eva-Lotta found herself in dire distress. She had to get hold of Anders and Kalle, and fast. She had an idea they were roaming about close by, hungry as wolves, waiting to see the burning lamp in her window as a sign that the coast was clear. But the coast wasn't clear. Nick didn't seem to want to leave. He insisted on telling Rasmus stories about when he was a young sailor, crossing the world's oceans, and Rasmus, the nitwit, was encouraging him.

It was urgent now, incredibly urgent! In less than

an hour Peters and Nick would set off and, under cover of darkness, get their hands on those precious documents.

Eva-Lotta could see only one way out—she let out the major catastrophe howl. It sounded precisely as dreadful as it was supposed to, and it almost scared the life out of Nick and Rasmus. When Nick had recovered, he shook his head and said:

'That just about puts the tin lid on it! No one in their right mind makes a noise like that!'

'That's how lonely wolves howl,' said Eva-Lotta. 'I thought you might like to hear it. It goes like this.' And she howled again, as ear-piercingly as before.

'Thank you, thank you, that's enough,' said Nick. And he was right. Because somewhere out there in the darkness a blackbird whistled. Now, a blackbird isn't usually in the habit of singing after nightfall, but Nick didn't appear to be surprised. Neither did Eva-Lotta. She was bursting with joy at Anders and Kalle's answer: 'We've heard you!'

But how would they get the important message about the documents? Pah! A knight of the White Roses always knew a way! Their secret language, the Robber language, had come in handy on more than one occasion, and so it did now.

Nick and Rasmus got another shock when all of a sudden Eva-Lotta broke out in a loud wail:

'*Sos-a-vov-e pop-ror-o-fof-e-sos-sos-o-ror-sos*

dod-o-coc-sos bob-e-hoh-i-non-dod bob-o-o-kok-coc-a-sos-e,' she sang over and over again, despite Nick's protests.

'Now just you listen to me,' he said finally. 'Put a sock in it. What are you caterwauling about?'

'It's an old native love song,' said Eva-Lotta. 'I thought you'd like to hear it.'

'I think it sounds like you've got a pain somewhere,' said Nick.

'*U ror gog c non tot,'* sang Eva Lotta, until Rasmus put his hands over his ears and said:

'Eeba-Lotta, can't we sing "Macdonald's Farm" instead?'

But in the darkness outside, Kalle and Anders stood and listened aghast to Eva-Lotta's message: *Save professor's docs behind bookcase! Urgent!*

If Eva-Lotta said it was urgent and had used the major catastrophe howl, it could only mean that Peters had found out, somehow, where the documents were hidden. They had to get there first.

'Quick,' said Anders. 'We'll borrow one of their boats.'

Without another word they pelted down the narrow track that led to the jetty. They stumbled in the darkness, scratched themselves on branches and pine needles, they were hungry and frightened and they imagined a crook was lurking behind every bush, waiting to leap out at them—but all of that meant nothing. The only important thing now was to make sure the professor's documents didn't end up in the wrong hands.

They experienced a couple of nerve-wracking minutes until they found a rowing boat that was unlocked. Any second they expected Blom or Nick to appear out of the gloom, and as Kalle slowly pushed the boat out from the jetty and picked up the oars, he had only one thought in his head: They're coming now. I know they're coming.

But no one came, and Kalle picked up speed. Soon they were out of hearing of the island, and he rowed so the water gushed around the oars. Anders sat silently at the back, thinking of when they had swum across. Was it really only yesterday morning? It felt like an eternity ago.

They hid the boat in a clump of reeds and ran to get the motorbike. They had left it in a tangle of undergrowth among some juniper bushes—where were those juniper bushes, for pity's sake, and how would they find them in the shadows?

Numerous precious minutes were wasted in a desperate search. Anders was so tense he started chewing his fingers. Where was that wretched bike? Kalle groped among the bushes and yes, here it was! He had found it. He wrapped his fingers fondly round the handlebars and quickly wheeled the bike out on to the forest track.

They had about a thirty-mile journey ahead of them. Kalle looked at his watch. The hands glowed in the darkness.

'It's half past ten,' he told Anders, who hadn't asked. It felt somehow monumentally important.

At that very moment Peters was saying exactly the same thing to Nick:

'It's half past ten. Time we got going.'

Thirty miles, twenty-five, twenty left to Lillköping! They were sweeping through the warm July night but to them the road seemed endless. Their nerves were on edge as they listened for the car that could be catching them up. Every instant they waited to be trapped in headlights closing in from behind, closing in and gliding past, and taking with them all hope for the documents which were so important.

'Lillköping eight miles,' Anders read aloud from a road sign. They were approaching familiar territory.

At about the same time, a black car was passing a different road junction.

'Lillköping sixteen miles,' read Nick. 'Step on it, boss!'

But Peters drove at precisely the speed that suited him. He lifted one hand from the wheel and offered Nick a cigarette, saying placidly:

'If I've waited this long, another half an hour won't hurt.'

Lillköping! The town is sleeping as safe and secure as ever. It's rather touching, think Kalle and Anders.

The motorbike roars along the well-known streets,

takes the road towards the castle ruins, and stops outside Eklund House.

But the black car still has a few miles to go before it reaches the road sign with its friendly: 'Welcome to Lillköping!'

'This is the most heart-stoppingly terrifying thing I have ever done,' whispers Anders, as they tiptoe onto the veranda. He feels the door cautiously. It's not locked. Those kidnappers must be complete birdbrains, leaving a door unlocked behind them, thinks Kalle. Fancy leaving doors wide open in a house where there are documents worth hundreds of thousands! But all the better—it saves a load of time! And he is acutely aware of how precious time is.

Behind the bookcase. Which bookcase? Doctor Eklund, who has let his house over the summer, is a man with tons of books and tons of bookcases. In the sitting room there are bookcases along every wall.

'This is going to take all night,' groaned Anders. 'Where shall we start looking?'

Kalle stops to think, even though time is short. But sometimes it pays to sacrifice a minute or two. What was it Rasmus had said to his dad? 'I crept up behind you the other evening when you thought I was asleep. That's when I saw . . .'

Where could Rasmus have been standing when he saw that? Most definitely not in the sitting room.

The bedrooms are upstairs. A little kid who couldn't sleep comes padding down the stairs, and even before his dad sees him Rasmus realizes something exciting is going on, and he stops. He must have been standing on the staircase out in the hall, thinks Kalle, and he heads straight for it.

Wherever he stands on the stairs, there is only one bookcase he can see through the open sitting room door. The one next to the writing desk.

He pelts back to the sitting room and together he and Anders start to drag the bookcase away from the wall. It scrapes loudly against the floor and the scraping is all they can hear. What they don't hear is the sound of the car pulling up outside.

Just a bit more and they can peer behind the bookcase. Holy moly—there it is! A brown envelope, well and truly stapled shut. Kalle's hands shake as he gets out his knife and starts to twist the staples open.

'I can't believe we made it in time,' whispers Anders, white as a sheet from the tension. 'I can't believe we actually made it!'

Kalle holds the valuable envelope in his hand. He stares at it breathlessly—it's worth a hundred thousand! Well, to tell the honest truth, it's probably priceless. Oh, what a moment of triumph, what a stonking great feeling of achievement!

Then they hear something! Something that strikes

them with terror. Shuffling steps on the veranda. A hand lifting the latch. The front door slowly opening.

The light from the desk lamp falls on their pale faces as they stare helplessly at each other. The fear practically makes them feel sick. They are caught like two rats in a trap. The people out in the hall are blocking the exit. The people out in the hall are not going to let anyone get past with a valuable brown envelope worth a hundred thousand.

'Quick, quick,' whispers Kalle. The stairs!'

It feels like their legs won't carry them, but by some superhuman effort they manage to run out into the hall and up the staircase.

Then everything happens so fast their brains freeze and their common sense disappears—disappears in the chaos, in the hubbub, where all they hear are frantic voices, swearing, and feet thudding up the stairs. Yes— help, help—footsteps right behind them!

There is the window with the curtain that waved at them so jauntily a thousand years ago. On the other side is a ladder, a way of escape, if only, if only . . . They tumble over the windowsill, out onto the ladder, climb— no, tumble—down it and run as they have never run before in their lives. They run even though they can hear the merciless voice up at the window—Peters' voice— that calls after them: 'If you don't stop, I'll shoot!'

But their common sense has abandoned them. All

they can do is race on, even though they should know their lives are at stake. They run and run until they feel their chests will explode.

And now they hear them again, those running feet, getting closer—where on earth can they find refuge from these hideous footsteps echoing in the night, these terrifying footsteps that will haunt their dreams for as long as they live?

Down to the town they race. It isn't far, but they are getting so very tired. And their pursuers are getting closer and closer. Nothing can save them, they are finished, any instant it will be too late!

Then they see him! They both see him. There is the first lamp post, and standing in its glow is a tall, familiar figure in a police uniform.

'Constable Björk, Constable Björk, Constable Björk!'

They shriek as if they are drowning at sea, and Constable Björk waves at them to calm down—you can't make a commotion like that in the middle of the night!

He walks towards them with no idea that right at this moment they love him more than their own mothers.

Kalle throws himself at Constable Björk, and wraps his arms around him, panting hard.

'Oh please, Constable Björk, arrest those crooks!'

He turns round and points, but the running footsteps have stopped. As far as they can make out in the darkness, there is not a single person to be seen. Kalle sighs—he doesn't know whether it's from relief or disappointment. There is no point chasing after kidnappers here, he realizes that. And he realizes something else. He can't tell Constable Björk what's going on. 'Don't get the police involved until Rasmus is safe'—the professor had been absolutely clear about that. Peters has been swallowed up by the night, it seems. No doubt he is on his way back to the car, which will whisk him back to his island—and to Rasmus! No, they can't tell the police, they can't go against the professor's orders. Even if deep down they suspect it would be the wisest thing to do.

'I see the master detective is in action again,' says Constable Björk with a smile. 'And where are those crooks, Kalle?'

'They got away,' puffs Anders, and Kalle stamps on his toes as a warning. But it's entirely unnecessary. Anders knows that when it comes to the business of crime, he has to let Kalle do the talking.

Kalle dismisses it all with a joke, and Constable Björk soon starts talking about something else.

'Well, you're a fine couple of lads,' he says. 'I bumped into your dad this morning, Kalle, and he was more than a little annoyed, believe me. Aren't you ashamed, running away like this? It's about time you came home.'

'Well, we're not home yet,' Kalle says. 'We're not quite home yet.'

12

If anyone had been passing Viktor Blomkvist's grocery shop at about 2 a.m. that morning, they would have thought a burglary was taking place. A torch was flashing behind the counter, and through the shop window two shadows could be seen tiptoeing backwards and forwards.

But nobody did have reason to wander past the shop at that time of night, and the two shadows remained undetected. Grocer Blomkvist and his wife, who slept in the room immediately above the shop, didn't hear anything either, because those shadows knew the art of moving silently.

'I want more sausage,' said Anders, with his mouth full. 'More sausage and more cheese.'

'Help yourself,' said Kalle. He had enough to do shovelling food into his own mouth.

They ate and ate. They cut thick slices of ham, and ate. They carved chunks off the best salami, and ate. They found a large, soft, wonderfully delicious loaf, and ate.

They peeled the foil off small triangles of cheese, and ate. They plunged their fists into the big box of raisins, and ate. They took bars of chocolate from the sweet counter, and ate. They ate and ate and ate. It was the feast of a lifetime, and they would never forget it.

'One thing I know for sure,' Kalle said, finally. 'I'll never eat a blueberry again, as long as I live.'

When he was full to bursting point, he crept upstairs. It was vital not to tread on the creaky stair. Through the years his mother had developed a remarkable ability to wake up at the sound of that creak when Kalle was the one who caused it—a massively supernatural phenomenon that researchers in psychology ought to study a little more closely, in Kalle's opinion.

Right now he didn't want to wake his mum, or his dad either, come to that. All he wanted to do was collect his backpack and sleeping bag and a few other camping things. If his parents woke up, too much time would be wasted trying to explain it all.

But Kalle's ability to avoid the creaky step had also developed through the years, and he returned safe and sound, and absolutely weighed down, to Anders in the shop.

At half past three in the morning, a motorbike was heading full tilt towards the road that wound its way to the sea.

On the counter in Mr Blomkvist's shop lay a piece of white paper torn from a pad, with the following message:

Dear Dad
You can keep my wages for this month because I have taken the following:
1 kilo salami
1 kilo cocktail sausages
1 ½ kilo ham
10 of those little cheese things, you know the ones I mean
4 loaves
½ kilo cheddar
1 kilo butter
1 box matches
10 bars of chocolate (those big ones)
1 ten-litre can of petrol from the store
2 tins cocoa
2 packets dried milk
1 kilo sugar
5 packets chewing gum
10 boxes firelighters
And possibly some other stuff I can't remember at the moment. I know you'll be angry, but if you knew the situation you wouldn't be, I'm sure. Please tell Eva-Lotta's dad and Anders' dad not to worry. Please don't be angry! I've always been a good son, haven't I?

Better stop now, before I get too upset.
   Lots of love to you and Mum,
   Kalle.
   PS You're not angry, are you?

Eva-Lotta slept restlessly that night and woke with a nagging feeling that something horrible was about to happen. She was anxious about Kalle and Anders. How had things turned out for them, and the professor's documents? Not knowing was awful, and she decided to have a real go at Nick the minute he arrived with breakfast. But when Nick did arrive he looked so bad-tempered that Eva-Lotta hesitated. Rasmus chirped a perky 'Good morning', but Nick took no notice of him and walked straight up to Eva-Lotta instead.

'Damned brat,' he said, with feeling.

'Oh, really?'

'You lie like a cheap watch,' Nick went on. 'Didn't you tell the boss you was on your own—you know, that night you got in the car?'

'The night you kidnapped Rasmus, you mean,' said Eva-Lotta.

'Yes, when we . . . Oh, get lost,' said Nick. 'But you did say you were alone, am I right?'

'Yes, that's what I said.'

'You were lying.'

'How do you mean?' asked Eva-Lotta.

'*How do you mean?*' mimicked Nick, turning red with rage. 'How? You had a couple of lads with you, admit it!'

'And what if I did?' Eva-Lotta answered cheekily.

'Yes, it was Anders and Kalle, I know that,' said Rasmus. 'Because they're in the White Roses, like Eeba-Lotta. And I'm going to be a White Rose too, so there.'

But Eva-Lotta had suddenly turned cold with alarm. Did Nick mean that Kalle and Anders had been caught? In that case, the game was up. She felt she had to know that very instant—she couldn't bear the uncertainty a minute longer.

'How do you know there were others with me?' she asked, as nonchalantly as she could.

'Because those flaming little delinquents have pinched those documents the boss was after—from right under their noses,' said Nick, glaring at her angrily.

'Hooray!' shouted Eva-Lotta. 'Hooray, hooray!'

'Hooray!' repeated Rasmus. 'Hooray!'

Nick turned to face him, and there was sadness in his eyes, sadness and concern.

'You can cheer now,' he said. 'But I got a feeling you won't be cheering much longer. Not when they take you out of the country.'

'What did you say?' cried Eva-Lotta.

'I said they're coming to take him abroad. A plane's coming tomorrow, to fetch him.'

Eva-Lotta gulped. Then she screamed and hurled

herself at Nick. She pummelled him wildly with her fists. She hit wherever she could reach, and shouted:

'You should be ashamed! It's wicked. You're wicked people—wicked shameful kidnappers!'

Nick didn't try to protect himself. He let her hit him. He just stood there, looking very tired all of a sudden. But then he hadn't had much sleep that night.

'Darn it! Why did those lads have to stick their noses in this?' he said eventually. 'Why couldn't the boss have got those documents he's so keen on, and put an end to all this misery?'

All this time Rasmus had been considering what Nick had said about flying to another country. He had weighed up the two possibilities. What was more fun—flying to a different country, or being a White Rose? When he had finished thinking he announced his decision.

'Do you know what, Nick? I don't think I'll fly to another country. I want to be a White Rose.'

He climbed up onto Nick's lap and told him in minutest detail how special it was to be a White Rose. He explained everything, from letting out a massive war cry to snooping about at night and fighting the Reds. It was vital that Nick understood all about the whole wonderful adventure of being a White Rose. Then he would understand why Rasmus couldn't travel abroad.

But when he had finished, Nick only shook his head gloomily and said:

'Afraid not, little Rasmus. You'll never be a White Rose. It's too late now.'

Then Rasmus slid off Nick's lap and walked away from him.

'Bleeping bellybuttons, you're so horrible,' he said. 'I *will* be a White Rose, so there!'

Nick walked towards the door. Someone outside was calling him.

Rasmus watched him go and realized he would have to be quick if he was going to get an answer to something he desperately wanted to know.

'Nick,' he said. 'If you spit from an aeroplane, how long does it take before the spit hits the ground?'

Nick turned and looked sadly at the little boy's eager face.

'I don't know,' he said. 'You can find out for yourself tomorrow evening.'

13

Eva-Lotta sat on her bunk bed, deep in thought. She chewed a strand of her hair and thought so hard her brain hurt. And she came to the conclusion it was hopeless. How could she, locked in this cage, be able to stop them putting Rasmus on a plane and taking him out of the country? And what kind of unscrupulous intention did Peters have? It was likely, thought Eva-Lotta, that now he had given up all hope of ever getting hold of those documents, he planned to force the professor to sit down and work out all his calculations again, and that meant taking him to some laboratory abroad, of course. And have Rasmus as hostage. Poor little Rasmus. So far nothing bad had happened to him, but how would he fare among a mob of bandits in a foreign country? In her mind Eva-Lotta saw the professor sitting at a desk, calculating like mad, while an evil prison guard raised his whip high over Rasmus's head and screamed: 'Get those calculations done, otherwise . . . '

It was a dreadful sight, and Eva-Lotta moaned softly.

'What's wrong with you?' asked Rasmus. 'And why isn't Nick coming to let me out so I can sail my bark boats?'

Eva-Lotta thought a bit more, and gradually an idea took shape in her head. She ran over to Rasmus eagerly.

'Rasmus, don't you think it's very warm today?'

'Yes, I do,' Rasmus agreed.

'Don't you think it would be super to go swimming?'

That did the trick.

'Yes!' shouted Rasmus, skipping in delight. 'Yes, let's go swimming Eeba-Lotta. I can swim five metres.'

Eva-Lotta clapped her hands in praise.

'Oh, I've simply got to see that,' she said. 'But it means when you ask Nick you'll have to nag and nag, otherwise we won't be allowed.'

'All right,' Rasmus said. He knew exactly how much he could achieve by using that method when necessary.

When Nick eventually turned up, Rasmus hurled himself at him.

'Nick, can we go swimming?' he began.

'Go swimming?' said Nick. 'What do you want to do that for?'

'It's so hot,' said Rasmus. 'We can go swimming when it's hot, can't we?'

Eva-Lotta kept quiet. She knew the wisest approach was to leave this entirely up to Rasmus.

'I can swim five metres,' Rasmus informed him. 'Do you want to see me swim five metres, Nick?'

'Well, I might,' Nick said slowly. 'But going swimming . . . No, I really don't think the boss would approve.'

'But I can't swim five metres unless I actually go swimming,' said Rasmus, with murderous logic. 'I can't swim on dry land, can I?'

He thought there was no arguing with that. Surely Nick couldn't be such a nincompoop he would turn down the chance to see Rasmus swim five metres? So he shoved his small hand into Nick's great big one and said: 'Come on, let's go!'

Nick glared menacingly at Eva-Lotta. 'You're going nowhere,' he said gruffly.

'Oh yes, Eeba-Lotta's coming. She's going to watch me swim five metres,' said Rasmus.

It was hard for Nick to resist that eager little voice. He despised his weakness, but now it had gone so far that all Rasmus had to do was put his hand in Nick's and look up at him with happy, expectant eyes, and Nick would do whatever he wanted.

'Oh, stone the crows, come on then,' muttered Nick.

⬛▬◀

This was everything she had dreamed of—running down the narrow path to the jetty, diving head first into the clear water as it glittered and rippled in the sunlight, stretching out on the jetty, shutting her eyes and thinking of absolutely nothing at all. But now, now that she had the chance, it seemed to Eva-Lotta nothing but a painful delay to putting her great plan into action. Rasmus, on the other hand, was delirious with joy. Like a happy little frog he scampered about in the shallow water by the beach. Nick sat on guard on the jetty, and Rasmus splashed him with water and laughed and shouted and jumped up and down, spraying water everywhere. He swam too, but then he was deadly serious and held his breath until he went red in the face. Afterwards he blew a huge puff of air and called to Nick:

'Did you see? Did you see me swim five metres?'

Perhaps Nick had, perhaps he hadn't.

'You're a funny little fish,' he said. It was the only comment he made about Rasmus' amazing ability to swim, but it sounded like praise.

Eva-Lotta lay on her back on the jetty and felt it being rocked by the waves. She stared up at the sky and continued repeating to herself: 'Keep calm, keep calm! It'll be all right!'

But she wasn't entirely convinced about that, and when Nick shouted: 'That's it, no more swimming!' she felt herself go pale with the tension.

'Oh, can't we stay a bit longer, Nick?' begged Rasmus. But Eva-Lotta knew she couldn't bear another minute, so she grabbed Rasmus's arm and said:

'No, Rasmus, come out now!'

Rasmus pulled away from her and looked pleadingly at

Nick. But for once Nick and Eva-Lotta were in agreement.

'Get a move on,' said Nick. 'We don't want the boss finding out about this.'

They had changed into their swimming gear behind some thick bushes, and Eva-Lotta grabbed the unwilling Rasmus by the hand and led him in that direction. In a flash she put on her clothes and then kneeled down to help Rasmus. His chubby little fingers had trouble with the buttons.

'It's not very easy, you know,' said Rasmus. 'Not when the buttons are at the back and I'm at the front.'

'I'll do them up for you,' said Eva-Lotta. And in a low voice trembling with nerves, she went on:

'Rasmus, do you really, really want to be a White Rose?'

'Oh, yes,' said Rasmus. 'And Kalle says—'

'Well, now you must do exactly as I say,' interrupted Eva-Lotta.

'What shall I do?'

'You must hold my hand and we're going to run away from here as fast as we can.'

'But Nick won't like that,' said Rasmus, looking worried.

'We can't worry about Nick right now,' whispered Eva-Lotta. 'We'll go and find the den Kalle and Anders have made . . .'

'Are you coming out or have I got to come and get

you?' yelled Nick from the jetty.

'Keep your hair on,' Eva-Lotta called back. 'We'll come when we're ready.'

Then she took Rasmus by the hand and whispered urgently:

'Run, Rasmus, run!'

Rasmus ran as fast as his five-year-old legs would let him, straight in among the fir trees. He tried as hard as he could to keep up with Eva-Lotta, so she would realize what a good White Rose he would be. And as he ran, he panted:

'At least Nick saw me swim five metres.'

14

The sun began to sink in the sky and Rasmus was tired. He didn't like this running-away business, and he hadn't liked it for some time.

'There are too many trees in this forest,' he said. 'When are we going to get to the den?'

Eva-Lotta wished she had an answer. She agreed with Rasmus that there were too many trees in this forest. And too many rocks to climb over, too many fallen branches that blocked their way, and too many prickly branches that scratched their legs. And not enough dens. One single little den was all she longed for, but it was nowhere to be found. Eva-Lotta felt her courage slowly fading. She had imagined it would be a simple thing to find the den, but now she was beginning to think they would never find it. And if at last they actually did—would Kalle and Anders be there? Had they even returned to the island after finding the documents? A thousand things could have happened to stop them. When you thought about it, perhaps they were alone on this island, she and

Rasmus—and the kidnappers. Eva-Lotta whimpered at the very idea. Please, please, Anders, *please* dear kind Kalle, be in the den, she begged silently and desperately. And let me find it soon, soon, *soon!*

'Blueberries! Miles and miles of blueberries!' said Rasmus, looking crossly at all the bushes that came up to his knees. 'I'd like some bacon.'

'I'm sure you would,' said Eva-Lotta. 'But bacon doesn't grow in the woods, unfortunately.'

'Bother,' said Rasmus, unhappy with this arrangement. 'And I want my bark boats too,' he went on, returning to a subject he hadn't dropped all day. 'Why couldn't I bring my bark boats with me?'

Little monster, thought Eva-Lotta. Here she was, caught up in a crazy adventure purely to save him from a terrible destiny, and all he did was moan about bacon and bark boats.

She regretted that thought immediately, and threw her arms around the boy. He was so little and so tired, of course. It was only natural he was whining.

'Sorry, Rasmus,' she said. 'I never thought about your bark boats . . .'

'Then I think you're horrible,' said Rasmus harshly.

He plonked himself down among the blueberry bushes. He wasn't going to walk any further. No amount of persuading helped. Eva-Lotta tried encouraging him.

'Perhaps the den is just around the corner,' she said.

'Perhaps we only need to walk a tiny bit further.'

But it was no good.

'Won't,' said Ramus. 'My legs are too tired.'

For a second Eva-Lotta wondered whether to give in to the tears that were welling up in her eyes, but then she gritted her teeth and sat down as well, leaning against a large rock. She pulled Rasmus close to her.

'Sit next to me and have a rest,' she said.

With a sigh, Rasmus stretched out on the cushiony moss and lay his head in Eva-Lotta's lap. He seemed absolutely determined not to walk another step. He looked up at Eva-Lotta sleepily, and she thought: Let him sleep for a while, it might make things easier. She took one of his hands in hers, and he didn't protest. Then she began singing to him. He blinked in an attempt to keep awake, and his eyes followed a butterfly that was flitting over the blueberry bushes.

'*Down in the forest the wild blueberries grow*,' she sang.

But Rasmus had a different idea.

'It would be better if you sang: 'Down in the forest the fried bacon grows,' he said. And then he fell asleep.

Eva-Lotta sighed. She wished she could go to sleep too. She wished she could fall asleep and then wake up at home in her own bed and discover she had dreamt the whole awful business. She sat there feeling miserable and worried, and very alone.

Then she heard voices in the distance. Voices that were getting closer, ones she recognized, and immediately afterwards the sound of branches cracking as someone trod on them. To think you could be so afraid and not die! No, you didn't die. You were paralysed by fear and couldn't move a muscle. Only your heart moved, wildly and painfully. It was Nick and Blom approaching through the woods, and Svanberg was with them.

There was nothing she could do. Rasmus was asleep on her lap. She couldn't wake him up and run off. There was no point. They would never make it in time. All she could do was sit here and wait to be caught.

They were so close now that Eva-Lotta could hear what they were saying.

'I've never seen Peters so flaming mad,' said Blom. 'And I'm not surprised, neither. You're such a knuckle-head, Nick.'

Nick growled.

'It's that blasted girl,' he said. 'I'd like to have a word or two with her. Just wait till I get hold of her.'

'Well, that shouldn't take too long,' said Blom. 'They have to be somewhere on the island.'

'Don't worry,' said Nick. 'I'll get them if I have to search behind every single bush.'

Eva-Lotta closed her eyes. They were ten steps away from her at the moment, and she couldn't bear looking at them. She closed her eyes and waited. Please let them discover her soon, so she could at last start crying. She had been waiting to do that for such a long time.

She sat with her back against the mossy rock, eyes closed, listening to the voices on the other side. So close, so scarily close! But then not quite so close. Fainter and fainter they became, until at last they were far away and it went strangely quiet. One small bird twittered in a bush, but that was the only sound she could hear.

For a long, long time she sat there on the moss. She didn't dare move. And anyway, she didn't want to move. She wanted to sit there and do nothing else for the rest of her life.

But eventually Rasmus woke up, and Eva-Lotta knew she had to pull herself together.

'Come on, Rasmus.' She said. 'We can't sit here any longer.'

She looked around her anxiously. The sun wasn't shining now. Big black clouds had piled up in the sky. It looked as if it there would be rain that night. The first drops were already beginning to fall.

'I want to go to my daddy,' said Rasmus. 'I don't want to be in the woods any more, I want to go to my daddy!'

'We can't go to your daddy right now,' said Eva-Lotta, in despair. 'We've got to try and find Kalle and Anders, otherwise who knows what will happen to us?'

She led the way through the blueberry bushes and Rasmus followed her, whimpering like a puppy.

'I'm hungry,' he said. 'And I want my bark boats.'

Eva-Lotta didn't answer. She kept silent. Then behind her she heard sobbing. She turned round and looked at the unhappy little figure standing among the blueberries with a trembling mouth and huge tears in his eyes.

'Oh, Rasmus, don't cry,' begged Eva-Lotta, even though that was what she most wanted to do herself. 'Don't cry, dear little Rasmus. Why are you crying?'

'I'm crying because . . .' hiccupped Rasmus. 'I'm crying because . . . my mummy is in hospital.'

Even someone who is going to be a White Rose has the right to cry when their mum is in hospital.

'She'll be coming out soon,' Eva-Lotta comforted him. 'You told me that yourself.'

'I'm crying about it anyway,' shouted Rasmus in a rage. 'Because I didn't remember to cry before . . . horrible Eeba-Lotta!'

The rain was getting heavier. It streamed down, cold and pitiless, and soon their thin clothes were soaked through. And all the time it was getting darker. The shadows loomed large among the trees. Very soon they wouldn't be able to see a step in front of them. They stumbled on, wet, hopeless, hungry and distraught.

Eva-Lotta wiped a few raindrops from her face. Perhaps there were a couple of tears there, too. She stopped, pulled Rasmus to her and said with a shaking voice:

'Rasmus, a White Rose has to be brave. We are both White Roses, you and me, and now we're going to do something that will be lots of fun.'

'What?' said Rasmus.

'We are going to crawl in under a fir tree and sleep there until morning.'

The future White Rose wailed as if someone had stuck him with a knife.

'I don't want to be in the woods when it's dark,' wailed Rasmus. 'I don't, I don't, I don't!'

'But you want to be in our den, don't you?'

It was Kalle's voice that spoke—Kalle's steady, calm voice, and it was more beautiful than an archangel's, thought Eva-Lotta. Not that she had ever heard or seen an archangel, but she was certain something similar in all its glory couldn't match up to Kalle as he came towards them through the darkness, shining his torch. Tears burst from Eva-Lotta's eyes, and this time she didn't hold them back.

'Kalle, is it you . . . is it really you?' she said, sobbing.

'How on earth did you get here?' Kalle asked. 'Did you escape?'

'You could say that,' said Eva-Lotta. 'We've been escaping all day!'

'We've escaped so I can be a White Rose,' Rasmus told him.

'Anders!' called Kalle. 'Anders, come and see a miracle.

Eva-Lotta and Rasmus are here!'

They sat on the soft branches inside the den and were very, very happy. It was still raining and the darkness outside among the trees was deeper than ever, but what did that matter? Inside it was dry and warm, they had changed out of their wet clothes, and life was no longer as nasty and unbearable as it had been only minutes before. The small blue flame of Kalle's camping stove flickered under the saucepan of hot chocolate, and Anders was cutting thick slices of bread.

'This is unbelievably wonderful,' sighed Eva-Lotta. 'I'm dry, I'm warm, and when I've eaten another three or four sandwiches I'll be full up as well.'

'I'd like some more ham,' said Rasmus. 'And hot chocolate!'

He held out his mug and Anders filled it to the brim again. Rasmus drank the warming chocolate in deep, satisfied gulps, only spilling one or two drops on Kalle's tracksuit which he had borrowed. It was so big he practically disappeared into its cosy, woolly warmth. He tucked his toes as far inside as he could, so that not even the tiniest bit of him would be on the outside, getting cold. Oh, it was lovely—the den, the tracksuit, the ham sandwiches—all of it!

'I'm very nearly a White Rose now, aren't I?' he asked, between bites.

'Yes, very nearly,' Kalle assured him. He was himself at this moment as content as anyone could possibly be. Think how well everything had worked out! Rasmus was safe, the documents were safe, and soon this nightmare would be over.

'First thing tomorrow we'll go to the boat and row Rasmus over to the mainland,' he said. 'Then we'll phone Constable Björk and get him to send the police to rescue the professor, and then the professor can have his documents . . .'

'And when the Red Roses hear they'll be so amazed their ears will drop off,' said Anders.

'Where are the documents, by the way?' asked Eva-Lotta.

'I've hidden them,' said Kalle. 'And I'm not going to tell you where.'

'Why?'

'It's best if only one person knows,' answered Kalle. 'We're not completely safe yet. And until we are, I'm not saying a word.'

'Nope, you're absolutely right,' said Anders. 'We can find that out tomorrow. Just think, tomorrow we'll be home again! That will be rather splendid, I think!'

Rasmus had a different opinion.

'I think it's much better in this den,' he said. 'I'd like to stay here for ever and ever and ever. We can stay a few more days, can't we?'

'No, thank you very much,' said Eva-Lotta, remembering those minutes with Nick and Blom in the woods. It was vital to get off the island as soon as the sun came up. For now they were protected by the darkness, but once it grew light they were doomed. Nick had said he would search behind every single bush on the island, and Eva-Lotta didn't intend staying until he had finished looking.

Eventually the rain stopped, and the tiny patch of sky visible through the den's opening began to be dotted with stars.

'I've got to get some fresh air before I go to sleep,' said Anders, and tumbled out. Immediately afterwards he called to the others:

'Come out here and you'll see something!'

'What can you possibly see in the dark?' Eva-Lotta called back.

'Stars,' said Anders.

Eva-Lotta and Kalle looked at each other.

'He's gone soft in the head,' said Kalle, looking concerned. 'We'd better go out.'

One by one they crawled out through the tight opening. Rasmus hesitated. It was light here inside the den—Kalle and Anders had hung their torches from the roof. It was light and warm inside, and outside it was dark. And he'd had enough of darkness.

But he didn't hesitate long. Wherever Eva-Lotta,

Kalle, and Anders were, that was where he wanted to be. He crawled out on all fours, like a small animal sticking its nose out of its burrow at night.

They stood close together in utter silence under the stars that twinkled against the deep, dark sky above their heads. They didn't feel like talking. All they did was huddle together, listening in the darkness. The deep rushing of the wind through the sleeping forest at night was something they had never heard before, or at least never listened to until now, and it was a soft and very special melody that had a strange effect on them.

Rasmus shoved his hand into Eva-Lotta's. This was like nothing he had ever experienced before, and it made him happy and afraid at the same time, so afraid that he wanted to hold someone's hand. But suddenly he knew he liked it. He liked the woods, even when it was dark and the wind was rustling through the trees like that. He liked the sound of the little waves lapping against the rocks. And best of all, he liked the stars. They shone so brightly, and one of them was twinkling kindly down at him. He tilted his head back and stared directly up at the star. And he squeezed Eva-Lotta's hand and said:

'Think how beautiful it will be inside heaven, when it's so beautiful on the outside!'

No one answered him. No one said a single word. But

finally Eva-Lotta crouched down and wrapped her arms around him.

'Well, Rasmus, bedtime for you,' she said. 'You'll be sleeping in a den in the woods—won't that be fun?'

'Oh, yes,' said Rasmus. He couldn't agree more.

And a moment later, after he had wriggled down into a sleeping bag beside Eva-Lotta, and lay there thinking how he was very nearly a White Rose, he drew a sigh of deep contentment. He snuggled closer to Eva-Lotta and felt very sleepy. He couldn't wait to tell his daddy how wonderful it was to sleep in a den at night. It was dark now because Kalle had switched off the torches, but Eva-Lotta was very near and the kindly star was probably still twinkling in the sky outside.

'There would be tons of room in this sleeping bag if you weren't taking up all the space,' said Anders, shoving Kalle in annoyance.

Kalle shoved him back.

'Pity we didn't think of bringing a bed for you,' he said. 'But never mind. Good night!'

Five minutes later they were sleeping peacefully, with not a single thought about the next day.

15

Soon they would be gone. In a matter of seconds they would leave and never return to this island. Kalle paused before jumping into the boat. He looked back at what had been their home for a few uneasy days and nights. There were the flat rocks they had swum from, looking so inviting in the morning sun, and behind the rocks, in a hollow, was their den. He couldn't see it from where he was, of course, but he knew it was there and that it was empty and abandoned and would never be home to them again.

'Are you going to take all day?' Eva-Lotta said, nervously. 'I want to get away from here. That's the only thing I want to do right at this moment.'

She was sitting on the seat in the back of the boat, with Rasmus next to her. She was keener than any of them to get away. Every second was precious, she knew that. All too easily she could imagine how enraged Peters would be over their escape, and how he would never give up trying to find them. That's why they had to hurry, they all knew that. Kalle too. He didn't dither any longer. With an athletic jump he landed in the boat where Anders was ready and waiting with the oars.

'Okay,' said Kalle. 'We're ready now!'

'Yep, all ready,' said Anders, and he started rowing. Then all of sudden he stopped and pulled a face.

'There's only one problem—I've left my torch behind,' he said. 'All right, all right, I *know* that was careless, but it'll only take a second to fetch it.'

He leapt onto the flat rocks and disappeared.

They waited quite patiently at first. Then after a while, enormously impatiently. Rasmus was the only one sitting calmly, dabbling his fingers in the water.

'If he doesn't come soon, I'll scream,' said Eva-Lotta.

'Knowing him, he's probably found a bird's nest or something,' said Kalle, annoyed. 'Rasmus, run and tell him the boat's leaving!'

Obediently, Rasmus jumped ashore. They watched him disappear over the rocks, bounding energetically like a young calf.

They waited. They waited and waited, staring at the outcrop of rocks where the people who had disappeared ought to be reappearing any second. But no one came. The rocks were as deserted as if no human had ever set foot there. An early-morning perch flipped in the water right beside the boat, and the reeds rustled softly along the shoreline. Otherwise it was quiet. Ominously quiet, they thought suddenly.

'What the heck are they doing?' Kalle said anxiously. 'I think I'd better go and check.'

'We'll both go,' said Eva-Lotta. 'I couldn't bear sitting here waiting all on my own.'

Kalle moored the boat and they leapt ashore. They ran up the rocks exactly as Anders had done. Exactly as Rasmus had done.

There was the den, down in the hollow. But there was no sign of anyone, and no voices either. Only an eerie silence . . .

'If this is one of Anders' pranks,' said Kalle as he crawled into the den, 'I'll teach him a . . .'

Kalle didn't finish his sentence. Eva-Lotta, two paces behind, heard a muffled cry, and she screamed wildly and desperately:

'What is it, Kalle? What is it?'

At that very moment she felt a hand grip the back of her neck, and she heard a familiar voice:

'You meddling little brat. Finished swimming now, have you?'

There stood Nick, his face red with rage and disappointment. And out from the den came Blom and Svanberg. They had three prisoners with them, and Eva-Lotta's eyes filled with tears when she saw them. This was the end. It was all over. Everything had been a waste of effort. She might as well lie down in the moss and die straight away.

It broke her heart to see Rasmus. He was in such distress, making desperate attempts to get rid of something that had been wedged into his mouth to stop him shouting. Nick hurried to help him, but this didn't result in any gratitude from Rasmus. As soon as his mouth was free he spat furiously in Nick's direction and shouted:

'I think you're horrible, Nick! Bleeping bellybuttons, you're so horrible!'

It was a bitter blow. Escaped prisoners on a chain gang in the jungle on their way back to Devil's Island must have felt like this, thought Kalle, and he clenched his fists as he walked. This was a real march of doom. They were all tied to a piece of rope, him and Anders and Eva-Lotta. Beside them walked Blom, the nastiest kind of prison guard, followed by Nick. He was carrying Rasmus, who didn't stop repeating how horrible he thought Nick was. Svanberg had seen to the rowing boat with all their supplies and was now on his way back to the kidnapper's lair with it.

Nick was clearly in a filthy temper. In reality he ought to be happy, returning to Peters with such a fine catch. But if he was, he went to a lot of trouble to hide it. He trudged behind them, muttering as he went.

'Confounded kids! What did you take the boat for? Did you think we wouldn't notice, eh? And when you had the boat, why did you stay on the island? Chumps.'

Yes, why *did* they, thought Kalle bitterly. Why hadn't they rowed to the mainland yesterday evening, even though Rasmus was tired and it was raining and dark. Why hadn't they got away from the island while there was still time? Nick was right—they were prize chumps! But how odd that he should be the one scolding them. He didn't seem particularly overjoyed that they had been caught.

'I don't think kidnappers are nice after all,' said Rasmus.

Nick didn't answer him. All he did was stare back angrily and carry on complaining.

'And why did you take those documents, eh? You two nitwits at the front—what were you doing, taking the documents?

The two nitwits didn't answer. And they didn't answer later, either, when Peters asked them the same question.

They were each sitting on a bunk in Eva-Lotta's cabin and were so downcast they didn't even have the strength to be scared of Peters, even though he did what he could to frighten them.

'You don't understand this kind of thing,' he said. 'And you should never have interfered. It'll be the worse for you if you don't tell me what you did with those documents last night.'

His dark eyes glared at them and he roared:

'Come on, out with it! What did you do with the documents?'

They didn't answer. It occurred to them that this would be the best way to drive Peters mad, because he suddenly propelled himself at Anders as if he was planning to murder him. He grabbed Anders by the head and shook him violently.

'Where are the documents?' he yelled. 'Answer me, otherwise I'll rip your head off!'

Then Rasmus intervened.

'Now you're really being horrible,' he said. 'Anders doesn't know where the documents are. Only Kalle knows. Because it's best only one person knows, Kalle says.'

Peters released his grip on Anders and looked at Rasmus.

'I see. Is that right?' he said, and immediately turned to Kalle.

'So you're Kalle, are you? Listen closely to me, my dear Kalle. You have exactly one hour to make up your mind. One hour, not a second longer. Then something will happen to you, something colossally unpleasant. Worse than anything you have ever experienced in your entire life. Have I made myself clear?'

Kalle looked superior, the way Master Detective Blomkvist always looked in these situations.

'Don't try to scare me, because it won't work,' he said.

But to himself he added silently: 'That's because I'm already about as scared as I could possibly be.'

Peters' hands were shaking as he lit a cigarette. He looked at Kalle to see if he could believe him, before going on:

'I wonder if you are intelligent enough to discuss this reasonably? If you are, then feel free to use your intelligence for a moment to understand what this is all about. It's like this: for various reasons, which I don't intend explaining to you now, I have become involved in something that's about as illegal as possible. I risk being imprisoned for life if I stay in Sweden, so I'm not planning on staying here a minute longer than necessary. I'm going abroad and I'm taking those documents with me. Now do you understand? You're not so stupid you can't understand that I'll do anything—and I mean anything—to find out where you hid them.'

Kalle nodded. He knew only too well that Peters would do whatever it took, and he also knew he would be forced to give in and betray the secret. How could a boy like him ever be able to stand against an utterly ruthless opponent like Peters?

He had been given an hour to consider, and he wanted to make the most of that hour. He wasn't going to give in before he had weighed up every available possibility.

'I'll think about it,' was all he said, and Peters nodded.

'Good. Think for an hour. And use your common sense, if you have any!'

He walked out, and Nick, who had been listening to the discussion with a grim expression, followed him to the door. But once Peters had left, Nick turned back and walked over to Kalle. He wasn't looking quite as furious as he had been all morning. In fact, he looked almost pleadingly at Kalle and said in a low voice:

'You can tell the boss where those papers are, can't you? Just to put an end to this misery. You can do that, can't you? For Rasmus' sake?'

Kalle didn't answer, and Nick left. In the doorway he turned and looked sorrowfully at Rasmus.

'I'll make a new bark boat for you later,' he said. 'A much bigger one . . .'

'I don't want a bark boat,' said Rasmus, ungratefully. 'And I don't think kidnappers are very nice.'

Then they were left to themselves. They heard Nick turn the key in the lock. After that they heard nothing except the wind in the treetops outside.

'Crumbs, the wind's getting up,' said Anders, after they had been sitting in silence for a long time.

'Yes,' said Eva-Lotta. 'I'm glad. I hope the storm is so bad it capsizes Svanberg's boat.'

Then she looked at Kalle.

'An hour,' she said. 'He's coming back in an hour. What are we going to do, Kalle?'

'You'll have to reveal where you've hidden them,' said Anders. 'Otherwise he'll kill you.'

Kalle scratched his head. 'Use your common sense' Peters had told him. And that was exactly what Kalle intended to do. Perhaps, if you used your common sense properly, there was a way of getting out of this mess.

'If only I could escape,' he said. 'It would be good if I could escape . . .'

'Yep. And if you could fly to the moon, that would also be good,' said Anders.

Kalle didn't answer. He was thinking.

'Listen,' he said. 'Doesn't Nick usually come with food about now?'

'Yes, I think so,' said Eva-Lotta. 'At least, we've always had breakfast about this time. Although, of course, Peters could be planning to starve us to death.'

'Not Rasmus,' said Anders. 'Nick wouldn't let Rasmus starve to death.'

'What if we were to throw ourselves at Nick, all of us at the same time,' said Kalle. 'When he comes with the grub. Could you hold him down long enough for me to escape?'

Eva-Lotta's face lit up.

'That would work,' she said. 'I'm sure that would work. Oho, I'm going to bash his head in. I've been longing to do that for ages.'

'I'll bash his head in too,' said Rasmus, gleefully.

But then he remembered his bow and arrows, and his bark boats, and added thoughtfully: 'But not very hard. Because he is quite nice, really.'

The others weren't listening. Nick could arrive at any minute and they had to be prepared.

'What are you going to do afterwards, Kalle?' asked Eva-Lotta. 'After you've escaped, I mean?'

'I'll swim over to the mainland and come back with the police, whatever the professor says. We've got to have help from the police. We should have done that long ago.'

Eva-Lotta shuddered.

'Yes, you're right,' she said. 'But no one knows what Peters is likely to do before they get here.'

'Shhh,' warned Anders. 'Nick's coming.'

Without a sound they rushed to the door and positioned themselves on either side. They heard Nick's footsteps getting closer and closer, and they heard the chink of plates on the tray he was carrying. They heard the key turn in the lock, and they tensed every nerve and muscle. Now. Now they were ready.

'Here I come with some scrambled eggs for you, little Rasmus,' called Nick, as he opened the door. 'Do you like—'

He never found out whether Rasmus liked scrambled eggs or not, because that very second they were on him. The tray fell with a crash to the floor and egg flew all over the place. They hung on tightly to his arms and legs, tipped him over, hit him, crawled all over him, sat on him, pulled his hair and banged his head against the floor. Nick growled like an injured lion and Rasmus skipped around the fighters, yelping happily. This was practically a War of the Roses, and he felt obliged to lend a hand. He hesitated briefly because Nick was his friend, after all, but after some consideration he walked over and gave him a hefty kick on the backside. Anders and Eva-Lotta fought as they had never fought before, and Kalle ran out of the door, quick as lightning. It was all over in a few seconds. Nick had the strength of a giant, and as soon as he had recovered from his surprise he freed himself with a couple of blows from his mighty fists. Angry and confused, he got up from the floor and immediately realized Kalle was missing. He flew to the door and tried to wrench it open. But it was locked. For a split second he stood there, staring stupidly at it. Then he threw himself as hard as he could at the door, but the planks were solid and didn't budge an inch.

'Who the hell has locked the door?' he shouted, incandescent with rage.

Rasmus jumped around, happy and excited.

'*I* did,' he shouted. 'It was *me*! Kalle ran and then I locked it.'

Nick grabbed his arm, hard.

'And where's the key, you little rogue?'

'Ow, that hurts,' said Rasmus. 'Let me go, horrible Nick!'

Nick shook him again.

'I said, what did you do with the key?'

'I threw it out the window,' said Rasmus. 'So there!'

'Bravo, Rasmus!' shouted Anders.

Eva-Lotta laughed out loud in delight.

'Now you can find out how it feels to be locked in, Nick,' she said.

'Yep, and it's going to be hilarious hearing what Peters has to say about this,' said Anders.

Nick slumped down heavily on the nearest bunk. He tried to arrange his thoughts. And when he had done that he burst out laughing, loudly and unexpectedly.

'Yes, it certainly is going to be hilarious hearing what the boss has to say,' he said. 'It certainly is.'

And then, just as suddenly, he became serious again.

'But this won't do at all. I've got to get hold of that lad before he causes any more trouble!'

'Before he fetches the police, you mean,' said Eva-Lotta. 'In which case, you'd better get a move on, dear Nick.'

16

There was a fresh westerly wind blowing and it was getting stronger every second. With a dull rushing sound it came over the tops of the pine trees and whipped up angry little white-topped waves in the bay that separated the island from the mainland. Panting after the violent fight and the crazy dash down to the sea, Kalle stopped at the water's edge and looked in despair at the foaming water. No mortal could swim across that without risking life and limb. Even with a small rowing boat it would be a dangerous undertaking. And of course he didn't even have a boat. He didn't dare get closer to the jetty in broad daylight, and naturally every boat would be locked.

For once Kalle was completely stumped. He was starting to get fed up with all the obstacles that kept piling up in their path. There was nothing he could do now except wait until the wind died down, and that could take several days. Where would he hide out during that time, and what would he live on? He couldn't stay in the den—they would look for him there—and he had no food because the kidnappers had taken it all. This was about as bad as it could get, thought Kalle, as he wandered aimlessly among the trees, anxious and alone. At any minute Nick could come chasing after him. He had to make a snap decision.

Then, through the sound of the wind, he heard loud cries for help coming from Eva-Lotta's cabin. He felt clammy with fear. Did it mean Peters was making the others pay in some horrible way because he himself had escaped? The very thought made his knees go weak under him. He simply had to find out what was going on up there.

Zigzagging through the bushes and trees, he returned the way he had come. The closer he got to the cabin, the easier it was to recognize the voices, and to his utter astonishment he realized it was Nick who was calling for help—Nick mainly, but Rasmus too. What in the name of creation were Anders and Eva-Lotta doing to Nick, to make him bellow like that? Kalle's curiosity made him want to investigate, even though it be would be extremely risky. But as luck would have it, the trees grew right up to the cabin, and with a little skill it would be possible to steal up to Eva-Lotta's window without being seen.

Kalle made his way between the trees. He was so close now he could hear Nick growling and swearing about something inside there, and he also heard the others' contented voices. Clearly Nick wasn't being hurt in any way, so what was he angry about? And why was he still in the cabin and not out looking for Kalle? And what was that shining in the grass right under Kalle's nose?

It was a key. Kalle picked it up and studied it closely. Could it be the key to Eva-Lotta's cabin? And if so, how had it ended up here? Another yell from Nick answered his questions.

'Peters! Come and help me!' shouted Nick. 'They've locked me in! Come and open the door!'

A grin spread over Kalle's face. Nick was locked inside with his prisoners. That truly was one point to the White Roses. Kalle shoved the key into his trouser pocket.

But at that very moment he heard Peters, Blom and Svanberg running over from the main house. He froze with fear. In no time at all they would be on his tail, he knew that, and they would search for him like they had never searched for anything before. Having Kalle on the loose was a deadly threat to Peters. Peters was clever enough to know that Kalle would do everything in his power to summon help, which was why nothing mattered more to Peters than preventing Kalle from leaving the island, at all costs. He would stop at nothing, Kalle knew, and that knowledge made him go pale under his suntan, as he lay anxiously listening to the footsteps thudding towards him. He had to find a hiding place, and he had to do it fast, within a few valuable seconds.

That's when he saw it, and it was right under his nose.

A fantastic hiding place, one they would never dream of searching. Under the concrete foundations of the cabin there was a gap with just about enough room to lie down more or less comfortably. It was only here, at the back of the cabin, that the foundations were high enough to crawl under, because the cabin was built on a slope running down to the sea. Tall grass and masses of purple willow herb grew here, blocking the gap from sight, just in case anyone had the bright idea of looking behind the cabin. Quick as a wink, Kalle wormed his way as far as he could under the cabin. They would be absolutely mad if they decided to look for him here, he reasoned. If they had any brains at all they would look for a runaway as far from his prison as possible, and not right under the prison floor.

He lay there listening to the earthquake as Peters realized the terrible truth, that Nick was locked in and Kalle had escaped.

'Go!' shouted Peters wildly. 'Go and find him! And don't come back without him or I won't be responsible for my actions!'

Blom and Svanberg went, and Kalle heard Peters putting a key, his own key, in the lock and opening the door. Then there was a second earthquake above his head. Poor Nick did his best to defend himself, but Peters was merciless. Nick had probably never experienced such a roasting in his life, and it went on until Rasmus decided to interrupt.

'You are *so* unfair, Mr Peters,' he said. Kalle could hear his determined little voice as clearly as if he had been in the same room. 'You are unfair *all* the time. It wasn't Nick's fault I locked the door and threw the key into the woods.'

Peters' only answer was a low growl. Then he bellowed at Nick:

'Get out and find the boy while I look for the key.'

That made Kalle jump, as he lay there under the foundations. If Peters started looking for the key he would get dangerously close to Kalle's hiding place—absolutely stonkingly too close!

This was a dog's life and no mistake. Every second you had to be ready to protect yourself from some new threat. Kalle thought fast and acted fast. The instant he heard Nick and Peters walk outside and lock the door, he left his hiding place. At lightning speed he crawled out and stood in waiting by the corner of the cabin. When he heard Peters come rushing out he stole along the other side of the cabin and up to the veranda, which Peters had just left. In the distance he could see Nick's back disappearing at great speed into the trees. Kalle plunged his hand into his trouser pocket and brought out the key. And to Anders and Eva-Lotta's utter astonishment he stepped in through the door less than a minute after Peters and Nick had vanished the same way.

'Now you keep quiet,' Eva-Lotta whispered to Rasmus, who looked as if he was just about to comment on Kalle's surprising return.

'But I haven't said anything,' Rasmus said indignantly. 'But if Kalle . . .'

'Shhh!' hissed Anders, and pointed a warning finger at Peters. He was poking about directly outside the window and was clearly exasperated that there was no key there.

'Sing, Eva-Lotta,' whispered Kalle, 'So Peters doesn't hear when I lock the door.'

So Eva-Lotta went and stood by the window, blocking the view in, and sang at the top of her voice:

'Do you think I'm downhearted? Oh no, not me . . .'

This did not appear to amuse Peters.

'Give it a rest,' he shouted irritably, and went on looking.

He was poking around with a stick in the grass and flowers under the window. It was obvious there was no key there. They could hear him swearing quietly to himself. Then he gave up searching and disappeared. They stood there, holding their breath, listening and waiting. Was he going away, or would he come back in and find Kalle? They listened until their ears practically stood out like loudspeakers. Listened and hoped, but then they heard Peters' footsteps on the veranda outside. He was coming! Oh, holy mackerel, he was coming! They stared at each other, totally defeated, totally pale, and totally unable to think a sensible thought.

Kalle recovered his ability to think a split second before it was too late. With a leap, he landed behind the screen that hid the wash stand. At the same moment the door opened and Peters strode in.

Eva-Lotta didn't move. She shut her eyes. Take him away, she thought, take him away because I won't be able to stand it. And if Rasmus decides to say something now, well . . .

'You'll get a thrashing as soon as I've got the time,' said Peters. 'When I get back you'll get such a thrashing you won't know what's hit you. And if you move even so much as an inch before I get back, it'll be so much the worse for you. Do you understand?'

'Yes, thanks,' said Anders.

Rasmus giggled. He hadn't heard a word Peters had said. He was obsessed with one thought only: Kalle was behind the screen! It was almost like playing hide and seek! Eva-Lotta watched his face anxiously. Shut up, Rasmus, shut up, she prayed. But Rasmus didn't hear her silent prayer. He giggled ominously.

'What are you grinning at?' roared Peters furiously.

Rasmus looked happy and secretive.

'You'll never guess who's . . .' he began.

'There are tons of blueberries growing on the island,' Anders blurted out. He dearly wanted to say something more sensible, but in his desperation this was all he could think of. Peters looked at him in disgust.

'Are you trying to be funny?' he said. 'Save yourself the trouble.'

'Ha ha, Mr Peters,' Rasmus carried on, unperturbed. 'You haven't a clue who's behind . . .'

'Blueberries are practically my favourite thing,' shouted Anders, and Peters shook his head.

'You're not the sharpest knife in the box, are you?' he said. 'But never mind. I'm going now. I only wanted to warn you: no more trouble!'

He walked towards the door, but stopped before he reached it.

'That reminds me,' he said to himself. 'I think I've got some razor blades in the wall cabinet.'

The wall cabinet! It was by the wash bowl. Behind the screen.

'Razor blades!' screeched Eva-Lotta. 'Oh, I've eaten them up . . . I mean, I've chucked them out the window. And I spat on the shaving brush.'

Peters stared at her.

'I feel sorry for your parents,' he said, and walked out of the door.

Then they were alone. They sat together on a bunk, the three of them, chatting quietly about what had happened. Rasmus sat on the floor at their feet, listening in interest.

'The wind is too strong,' Kalle said. 'We can't do a thing until it dies down.'

'Sometimes it blows nine days in a row,' said Anders, by way of encouragement.

'What will you do while you're waiting?' Eva-Lotta asked.

'I'll have to lie under the foundations with the other woodlice,' said Kalle. 'But after Nick's done his last round for the evening, I'll come back here to eat and sleep.'

Anders laughed.

'This is so good I wish we could do it again with the Reds,' he said.

They sat there for a long time, listening to the cries and shouts from the woods as Peters, Nick and Blom searched for Kalle.

'You can look,' Kalle said fiercely. 'You won't find anything except blueberries.'

Evening arrived and it became dark. Kalle couldn't lie under the cabin a moment longer. He had to get out and move his arms and legs before they withered away. It was too early to join the others in the cabin. Nick hadn't done his evening rounds yet. Silently and cautiously, Kalle crept out and walked about in the darkness. How wonderful it was to be able to move!

He could see a light shining up in the bigger house where Peters was. A window was open and he heard a low murmur of voices. What were they talking about in there? Kalle felt his sense of adventure begin to stir. If he crept up to that window without a sound and stood underneath it, perhaps he would hear a couple of things that could be handy to know.

He padded closer, one step at a time, listening anxiously between each step. Finally he was standing directly below the window.

'I'm sick and tired of this,' he heard Nick say irritably. 'I am well and truly sick and tired, and I don't want to be a part of it any more.'

Peters answered him coldly:

'I see, you don't want to be a part of it any longer! And why not, if I may ask?'

'Because something's wrong,' Nick said. 'Before, all I ever heard was talk about the *cause*, how they'd do whatever it took for the sake of the *cause*, or so they told me. Poor ignorant sailor that I am, I believed in that claptrap. But I don't believe in it no more. It ain't right to treat kids like this, however good it is for the *cause!*'

'Watch your step, Nick,' said Peters. 'Surely I don't have to tell you what happens to people who back out?'

There was a short silence before Nick answered sulkily:

'No, no, course not. I know that only too well.'

'That's all right, then,' Peters went on. 'And I'm warning you: don't try anything stupid. You're talking like a fool. I wouldn't be surprised if you let that kid escape deliberately.'

'Now hang on a minute, boss,' said Nick, angrily.

'No, of course. Even you couldn't be that stupid,' said Peters. 'Even you must be aware what it means for us now he's done a runner.'

Nick didn't answer.

'I've never been this afraid in all my life,' Peters continued. 'And if that plane doesn't get here soon, it'll be curtains for us, believe you me!'

Plane! Kalle pricked up his ears. What plane were they expecting?

His thoughts were interrupted. Someone came walking along in the darkness, someone with a torch. He was coming from the direction of the tiny cabin that lay below the professor's rocky hill. It must be Blom or Svanberg, thought Kalle, and he leaned in close to the wall.

But he had no need to be afraid. The man with the torch walked on up to the big house, and a moment later Kalle heard him talking inside with the others.

'The plane gets here at seven tomorrow morning,' Kalle heard him say, and he recognised Blom's voice.

'I'm heartily glad to hear that,' said Peters. 'I really need to get away from here. Let's just hope the weather allows them to land.'

'No problem. The wind's dropped, more or less,' said Blom. 'They want a new report before they set off.'

'Well, give them one,' said Peters. 'Here in the bay it's not blowing hard enough to stop them landing. And you, Nick, make sure the kid's ready by seven!'

'The kid'—that was Rasmus, of course. Kalle clenched his fists. So, that was how it would end! Rasmus would be taken away. He would be gone long before Kalle had time to get any help. Poor, poor Rasmus, where were they taking him? Oh, it was despicable!

It was exactly as if Nick had heard Kalle's thoughts.

'Despicable, that's what it is,' he said. 'Poor little tyke, he hasn't done any harm. Well, I'm not helping. The boss can put him on the plane himself.'

'Nick,' said Peters, and his voice sounded terrifyingly cold. 'I've warned you once, and I'm warning you again for the last time. Make sure the kid is ready at seven o'clock!'

'Hell's bells, boss,' said Nick. 'You know as well as I do that the kid will never get out of this alive. Not the professor, neither.'

'I wouldn't be so sure about that,' Peters said. 'If the professor would only show a little common sense . . . but that's got nothing to do with it!'

'Hell's bells,' said Nick again.

Kalle felt a lump in his throat. He was so sad. It seemed so hopeless, all of it. They had tried, they had really tried with every ounce of their strength to help Rasmus and the professor. But it hadn't done any good.

Those wicked people had won the last round after all. Poor, poor Rasmus!

Kalle stumbled through the darkness, filled with despair. He must try to make contact with the professor, let him know about the plane that was going to come in to land like a gigantic bird of prey first thing tomorrow and set its claws in Rasmus. The seaplane which would be landing on the water down in the bay as soon as Blom had reported that the wind had dropped enough . . .

Kalle screeched to a halt. How was Blom going to report that? How on earth was he going to do it? Kalle whistled. Of course—there must be a radio transmitter somewhere. Naturally there was a radio transmitter, every spy and villain needed one, to keep in contact with other countries.

A small idea began to grow in Kalle's brain. A radio transmitter—that was precisely what he needed right now! Thunderation, where was that transmitter? He had to find it! Maybe, just maybe there was some hope left after all!

That tiny cabin—the one Blom had come from! There it was. A weak light streamed through the window. Kalle trembled with excitement as he stole closer to look. There was no one to be seen. But—wonder of wonders— the radio transmitter was there. Yes, it was there!

Kalle felt the door. It was unlocked. Thank you, thank you, Blom! With a bound Kalle was over by the transmitter and gripping the microphone. Was there anyone out there in the big wide world who could hear him? Was there anyone who would understand his desperate cry?

'Help, help,' he pleaded, in a low, trembling voice. 'Help! It's Kalle Blomkvist here. If anyone is listening, please phone Constable Björk . . . I mean, ring the police in Lillköping and tell them to come to Kalvön and rescue us. Kalvön is the name of the island and it's roughly thirty miles south-east of Lillköping and this is urgent because we've been kidnapped. Get here fast, otherwise who knows what will happen to us? Kalvön is the island and—'

Was there anyone out there in the whole wide world listening to that transmitter? Anyone wondering why it had suddenly gone quiet?

Kalle was wondering too—wondering what kind of train had run him over and why his head was hurting so badly. But then he sank into a black hole and stopped wondering. With the last dregs of his consciousness he heard Peters say, in a voice filled with hate:

'I'll murder you, you little vandal! Nick, come here and carry him to the others!'

17

'We've got to have a think,' said Kalle, carefully feeling the bump on the back of his head. 'Or rather, you'll have to think. My brain seems to have come loose.'

Eva-Lotta fetched another wet towel, which she wrapped around his head.

'There,' she said. 'Now lie still and don't move.'

Kalle had nothing against lying still. After the thrills and spills of the past four of five days and nights, a soft bed felt wonderful. And it felt nice, if a bit idiotic, to be looked after by Eva-Lotta.

'I'm already thinking,' said Anders. 'I'm trying to think if there's anyone I know who I hate more than Peters, but I can't come up with anyone. Not even that woodwork teacher we had last term. He was a real sweetheart, now I come to think about it.'

'Poor Rasmus,' said Eva-Lotta. She picked up the candlestick and walked over to Rasmus' bed. He was sleeping very peacefully, as if there was no evil in the world. In the flickering candlelight he looked more angelic than ever, thought Eva-Lotta. His face had lost weight and his cheeks, under his long dark eyelashes, were so thin. The babyish mouth that used to give away so many secrets was now indescribably touching as he slept. He looked so little and defenceless that all Eva-Lotta's maternal instincts rushed painfully to her heart when she thought about the plane that would be taking him away the next morning.

'Is there really nothing we can do?' she said despondently.

'I'd like to lock Peters up with some kind of infernal machine,' Anders said between gritted teeth. 'A little machine from hell that suddenly goes *click* and it's goodbye, villain!'

Kalle laughed. He had managed to think of something.

'Talking about locking up,' he said. 'We're not locked in at all. I've got the key, haven't I? We can escape whenever we like.'

'Jumping Jehosaphat!' said Anders, in amazement. 'Of course, you've got the key! So what are we waiting for? Come on, let's scram!'

'No, no, no,' said Eva-Lotta. 'Kalle must lie still. After a whacking great bash on the head like that he mustn't even lift his head off the pillow.'

'We'll wait a few hours,' said Kalle. 'If we try to take Rasmus into the woods now, he'll scream blue murder and the whole island will hear. And we'll sleep better here than under a bush in the woods.'

'You're talking so sensibly anyone would think your brain has started working again,' said Anders. 'I know what we'll do. We'll sleep for a couple of hours and then scarper about five. And we'll have to hope and pray it's calmed down enough by then so one of us can swim to the mainland and get help.'

'Yes, otherwise it will all go down the drain,' said Eva-Lotta. 'We can't stay hidden on the island indefinitely. I know what it's like, being in the woods with Rasmus without any food.'

Anders wriggled down into the sleeping bag which Nick had let him keep out of the goodness of his heart.

'Bring me coffee in bed at five,' he said. 'I'm going to sleep now.'

'Goodnight,' said Kalle. 'I have a feeling rather a lot is going to happen tomorrow.'

Eva-Lotta lay down on her bunk. She clasped her hands behind her head and stared up at the ceiling where an annoying fly was buzzing around, making small thuds every time it bumped into something.

'Anyway, I quite like Nick,' she said.

And then she rolled over onto her side and blew out the candle.

Kalvön, thirty kilometres south-east of Lillköping, is

a huge expanse of land for anyone wandering around in the woods searching for a den, but for anyone approaching it from the air, the island it is only a tiny, tiny green dot in a blue sea full of many other tiny, tiny green dots. From somewhere far, far away a seaplane has just started its journey towards the little island lying there off the coast among a thousand others. The seaplane has powerful engines and it doesn't take many hours for it to reach its destination. They roar monotonously and very soon the inhabitants of Kalvön can hear the droning sound that slowly gets louder and grows to a terrible row as the machine lands in the bay.

The sea is heaving with billowing waves after the storm, but the bay is out of the wind and with a final ear-splitting roar the machine rushes over the surface and comes to a standstill by the jetty.

Only then does Kalle wake up. And at the same time he realizes that the roaring sound isn't coming from the Niagara Falls at all, as he had dreamed, but from the plane that has come to collect Rasmus and the professor.

'Anders! Eva-Lotta! Wake up!'
It sounds like a wail and immediately brings the others out of their beds and up onto their feet. They realize the seriousness of the situation. Now they need nothing less than a miracle if they are going to get away in time.

Kalle throws a look at the clock as he pulls Rasmus from his bed. It's only 5 a.m. What's going on? The plane is arriving two whole hours before it's due!

Rasmus is tired and doesn't want to get up at all, but they ignore his protests. Eva-Lotta forces him into his dungarees and he hisses like an angry kitten. Anders and Kalle stand and watch, fidgeting impatiently. Rasmus tries to pull away until finally Anders grabs him roughly by the scruff of the neck and roars:

'You don't think a whining little whippersnapper like you will ever be a White Rose, do you?'

That does the trick. He shuts up and in a no-nonsense way Eva-Lotta gets his trainers on. Kalle crouches down beside him and pleads:

'Rasmus, we're escaping again! We might go to that nice den, you know the one I mean? You must run as fast as you can!'

'I've never known anything like it,' says Rasmus, because that's what his daddy sometimes says. 'I've never known anything like the pranks you get up to.'

They are ready at last. Kalle rushes to the door and listens with frayed nerves. But there is not a single sound. It seems their way is open. He feels in his pocket for the key. Feels and feels . . .

'For goodness' sake,' says Eva-Lotta. 'Don't tell me you've lost the key!'

'It's *got* to be here,' says Kalle. He is so nervous his

hands are shaking. 'It's got to be here!'

But however deep he digs, his pocket is empty. He has never felt anything as empty as that pocket. Anders and Eva-Lotta say nothing, but they chew their fingernails anxiously.

'What if it fell out when they carried me in here yesterday?' says Kalle.

'Yes, why wouldn't it fall out, seeing as everything else has gone so horribly wrong,' says Eva-Lotta bitterly. 'What else can you expect?'

The seconds tick by. The precious seconds. They search the floor frantically, all except Rasmus. He has started playing with his bark boats, and they sail over Kalle's bunk as if it was the Pacific Ocean. There's a key in the middle of the Pacific Ocean, and Rasmus picks it up and pretends it's the captain of a boat called *Hilda of Gothenburg*. Nick was the one who thought up such a fine name. It is the name of a boat Nick sailed on once in his seafaring days a long, long time ago.

The seconds tick by. Anders and Kalle and Eva-Lotta search and search and are so nervous they could scream. But Rasmus and the captain of *Hilda of Gothenburg* aren't nervous, not a bit. They sail over the Pacific Ocean and are having such a lovely time, right up until Eva-Lotta with a shriek pulls the captain from his post, leaving *Hilda of Gothenburg* to drift aimlessly among the waves.

'Quick, quick,' calls Eva-Lotta, handing Kalle the key. He takes it and is about to put it in the lock when he hears something, and throws the others a desperate look.

'It's too late, they're coming,' he says.

In actual fact it is a pointless remark, because he sees on the ashen faces of the others that they have heard, too.

The person coming in is in a hurry, a tearing hurry. They hear the key in the lock, the door is wrenched open, and Peters is there looking absolutely wild. He rushes over to Rasmus and grabs him by the arm.

'Come on,' he says, abruptly. 'Hurry up and come with me!'

But by this time Rasmus is tired of all this pulling and pushing about. First the Captain of the 'Hilda', and now him!

'I won't!' he says furiously. 'Go away, you horrible old Mr Peters!'

Then Peters bends down, picks Rasmus up and holds him tightly. He walks towards the door. The prospect of being separated from Eva-Lotta and Kalle and Anders terrifies the life out of Rasmus. He struggles and screams:

'I won't . . . I won't . . . I won't!'

Eva-Lotta covers her face with her hands and cries. It is all so horrible. Kalle and Anders are also finding it hard to control their feelings. They stand motionless and despairing, and hear Peters lock the door, hear him walk away, hears Rasmus' cries as they gradually die away.

Suddenly Kalle comes to life. He gets out his key again. They have nothing else to lose. And at the very least they have to see the sorrowful end of the story, so they can tell it to the police later. Later, when it's too late and Rasmus and the professor have disappeared somewhere where the Swedish police can't do a single thing to help them.

They crouch behind some bushes near the jetty and follow the dramatic events with tears stinging their eyes.

There is the seaplane. And here come Blom and Svanberg with the professor between them. The prisoner, who has his arms tied behind him, isn't trying to resist. He seems almost apathetic. He steps submissively into the plane and sits there, staring blindly ahead. Then Peters come racing down from the big house. He is still carrying Rasmus, and Rasmus is still struggling as wildly and shrieking as loudly as before.

'I won't ... I won't ... I won't!'

Peters walks rapidly down the long jetty, and when the professor catches sight of his son he looks more inconsolable than they thought anyone could look.

'I won't ... I won't ... I won't!' shrieks Rasmus. Peters slaps him hard to make him shut up, but Rasmus screams worse than ever.

Suddenly, there on the jetty is Nick. They hadn't seen him coming. He is red in the face, and his hands are clenched. But he doesn't move. He only stands still, looking after Rasmus with a look of indescribable sorrow and sympathy.

'Nick!' screams Rasmus. 'Help me, Nick! Nick, can't you hear me . . .'

The frail little voice breaks. He is crying desperately and reaching out his arms to Nick who is always so kind and makes such wonderful bark boats.

Then something happens. Like a gigantic crazed animal Nick comes rushing along the jetty. He catches up with Peters right beside the seaplane and with a cry, tugs the little boy towards him. He punches Peters on the chin, making him stagger. And before Peters has found his balance, Nick is off and running at full speed back down the long jetty.

Peters screams after him, and Eva-Lotta shudders. She has never heard a more hideous scream.

'Stop, Nick! Otherwise I'll shoot!'

But Nick doesn't stop. He holds Rasmus even tighter and runs towards the forest.

One shot rings out, then another. But evidently Peters is too rattled to aim straight. Nick runs on and soon disappears among the trees.

The screech Peters gives is barely human. He signals to Blom and Svanberg to follow him, and all three tear after the runaways.

Kalle and Anders and Eva-Lotta stay where they are behind the bushes, staring in terror at the forest. What is going on in there among the trees? It feels almost worse when they can't see anything, and all they can hear is Peters' dreadful voice shouting and swearing and gradually getting fainter and fainter as he goes further into the trees.

Then Kalle turns his gaze in the other direction. Towards the plane. The professor is sitting inside, guarded by the pilot. But no one else.

'Anders,' whispers Kalle. 'Can I borrow your knife?'

Anders pulls his pocket knife out of the holder on his belt.

'What are you planning to do?' he asks.

Kalle feels the edge of the blade.

'Sabotage,' he says. 'Sabotage the plane. That's all I can come up with right now.'

'Well, that's not a bad idea for someone with a dent in their head,' Anders whispers encouragingly.

By this time Kalle has thrown off his clothes.

'Give a really loud yell in a couple of minutes,' he says to the others. 'To make the pilot look in your direction.'

Then he sets off. He makes his way in a wide curve between the trees and gets close to the jetty. And when Anders and Eva-Lotta let out a wild yell he runs the remaining few metres and glides down into the water.

He guessed right. The pilot looks warily in the direction of the noise and doesn't see the Kalle streak past like an arrow.

Kalle swims underneath the jetty. Silently—just like they have practised hundreds of times in the Wars of the Roses. Soon he has reached the end of the jetty and is alongside the seaplane.

He peers up cautiously and sees the pilot through the open cabin door. He also sees the professor and, more importantly, the professor sees him. The pilot is staring blindly at the forest, noticing nothing. Kalle raises the knife and mimes a few stabbing movements so the professor will understand what he is going to do.

And the professor does understand. He also realizes what he's got to do himself. If Kalle attacks the plane with that knife it will make some noise and the pilot is bound to hear it. Unless, of course, he is distracted by an even louder noise coming from somewhere else.

The professor decides the noise is going to come from him. He starts shrieking and ranting and stamping on the floor. Let the pilot think he's gone stark staring mad—it's an absolute miracle he isn't mad already!

The pilot jumps in fright when the prisoner lets out his first shriek. It scares him because it was so unexpected. Then the fear turns to anger, because he let himself be afraid.

'Shut your trap,' he says, with a strange kind of accent. He doesn't speak a lot of Swedish, but he knows that much at least.

'Shut your trap,' he says, and his accent makes him sound relatively friendly.

But the professor shouts and kicks worse than ever.

'I'll cause as much trouble as I like,' he yells, and at that moment it feels a fantastic relief to be able to kick out and cause a rumpus. It relieves the pressure he's been under.

'Shut your trap or I'll punch nose off face!'

But the professor goes on yelling, and down in the water Kalle works quickly and methodically. He is on the plane's left side and he plunges the knife into the float over and over again, puncturing and twisting anywhere he can reach. Water starts seeping in through the many small holes. Kalle is very satisfied with his work.

Ha, you could certainly do with some impenetrable metal in situation like this, he thinks to himself as he swims back under the jetty.

'Shut your trap,' repeats the pilot, still sounding very friendly. And this time the professor obeys.

18

It is Tuesday the 1st of August, and six o'clock in the morning. The sun is beaming down on Kalvön, the sea is blue, the heather is in bloom and the grass is thick with dew. Eva-Lotta is standing in a bush, being sick. Is she going to feel sick for the whole of the rest of her life every time she remembers this morning? Will they ever be able to forget it, she and the others who were with her?

It was that pistol shot. Somewhere deep inside the forest, someone fired a shot. Far away, quite far away. But in the stillness of this particular morning it resounded loudly and forebodingly, and the sound hit her eardrums so tortuously clear and sharp, it made her feel sick and she had to throw up.

They didn't know what the bullet had hit or what its intended target had been. They only knew Rasmus and Nick were there in the forest together with a ruthless person armed with a gun. And there was nothing they could do except wait. But no one knew what they were waiting for. Waiting for something—anything—to happen that would change this unbearable situation. An endless wait! It felt like a lifetime. Perhaps it will be like this for all eternity—early morning sun on a long jetty, a seaplane bobbing in the water, a little white wagtail hopping through the clumps of heather, red ants crawling over the rocks behind the bushes where you are lying, waiting. And in the forest, nothing but silence. Is it really going to last for all eternity . . . ?

Anders has good ears. He is the first to hear it.

'Listen,' he says. 'I think I can hear a motor boat!'

The others listen. Yes, it's true—the very faintest throb of engines can be heard out over the water. In this isolated group of islands that seem to be abandoned by God and any form of human life, this faint throbbing is the first sound to reach them from the outside world. During their five days on the island they haven't seen any other people, not a motor boat, not even a little rowing boat with someone fishing. But now there is a motor boat out there in the bay. Is it heading their way? Who knows? There are so many bays and inlets here, there are a thousand chances the boat is going in an entirely different direction. But if it is coming this way then they can race out onto the jetty and shout at the top of their lungs: 'Come here, come here, before it's too late!' But what if there's only a crowd of happy holidaymakers in the boat, waving and laughing and passing by, not bothering to come closer and find out what's going on?

The tension and the uncertainty are getting harder to cope with every second.

'We'll never be normal human beings again after this,' says Kalle.

The others aren't listening. They are not aware of *anything* except that rumbling sound coming from the sea. And it's coming nearer. Soon they can see the boat, far, far away. Or boats, rather, because there are two of them!

But someone is coming from the trees. It's Peters. And, hot on his heels, Blom and Svanberg. They are running towards the seaplane as if their life depended on it. Maybe they have also heard the motor boats and are feeling scared? There is no sign of Rasmus and Nick. Does that mean . . . No, they can't bear to think what that means! Their eyes follow Peters. He's at the plane now, he's climbing aboard, to where the professor is. It looks as if there is no room for Blom and Svanberg. They hear Peters yelling: 'Hide yourselves in the forest for now. You'll be picked up this evening!'

The propeller whirs. The plane begins to dart backwards and forwards over the water, and Kalle bites his lip hard. Now he'll find out whether his sabotage has worked or not.

Backwards and forwards. Backwards and forwards over the water. But the plane doesn't take off. It tilts sharply to one side, tilts more and more, until it tips right over.

'Hurray!' shouts Kalle, forgetting everything else. But then he remembers that the professor is on board the plane too, and when he sees it start to sink he gets worried.

'Come on!' he calls to the others. And they charge out from the bushes, a wild little band of warriors who have been lying in wait all this time.

The plane has sunk out in the bay. There is no sign of it now. But people are swimming in the water. They count, anxiously—yes, there are three of them.

Then suddenly the motor boats are here. Yikes! Who's that standing in the front of one of them?

'Constable Björk! Constable Björk! Constable Björk!'

They shout so hard they almost snap their vocal chords.

'Oh, it's Constable Björk,' sniffs Eva-Lotta. 'Oh, bless his heart, thank goodness he's here!'

'And look at the backup he's got with him!' shouts Kalle, delirious with happiness and relief.

It's pandemonium out there in the bay. All they can see is a swarm of uniforms and lifebuoys being thrown into the water and people being hauled out of the water. They watch as at least two are pulled out. But where is the third?

The third is swimming ashore. It seems he doesn't want any help. He's planning to save himself, by the look of things. One of the motor boats steers a course after him, but he's got a head start.

Now he reaches the jetty. He grabs it, clambers up and runs with long, squelching strides directly towards Anders and Kalle and Eva-Lotta. They have crawled behind the bushes again, because the running man is desperate and they are afraid of him.

Now he is right beside them and they see his eyes full of rage and disappointment and hatred. But he isn't using his eyes, he doesn't see the little band of warriors behind the bushes. He isn't aware that he has his worst enemies so close. But just as he jogs past, a boy's leg, thin and knobbly, pokes out and trips him up. Cursing, he falls flat on his face in a clump of heather. And now his enemies are on top of him, all three of them at once. They force him to the ground, holding tight to his arms and legs, pressing his head into the ground and shouting:

'Constable Björk, Constable Björk, come and help!'

And Constable Björk comes and helps. Of course he does. He has never yet let his friends down, the brave knights of the White Roses.

But in the woods, a man is lying on his back in the moss, and a small boy is sitting beside him, crying.

'Look, Nick, you're bleeding,' says Rasmus. There is a red stain on Nick's shirt and it is spreading fast. Rasmus points at it with a dirty little finger.

'Bleeping bellybuttons, that Mr Peters is so horrible! Did he shoot at you, Nick?'

'Yes,' says Nick, and his voice is very weak and strange. 'Yes, he shot at me . . . but don't you upset yourself about that . . . You're safe, that's the main thing.'

He is only a poor ignorant seaman, and he's lying there thinking he's about to die. And he is glad. He has done so many stupid things in his life, and he's glad the last thing he did was something right and proper. He has saved Rasmus. He doesn't know that yet, as he lies there, but at least he knows he tried. He knows he ran until he felt his heart would burst and he couldn't run any further. He knows he held Rasmus tight in his arms, right up until the bullet was fired and he fell, and Rasmus scuttled like a scared little hare in among the trees, and hid. But now the scared little hare is back with Nick again, and Peters has disappeared. He was in such a hurry to get away, it seems he didn't dare stay and look for Rasmus. And that's why they are alone now, Nick and this little mite who is sitting beside him and crying and is the only person Nick has ever cared anything about. Nick hasn't the faintest idea how that happened. He can't remember how it started . . . Perhaps already the first day, when he had given Rasmus the bow and arrows and the little boy had thrown his arms around Nick's legs and said:

'Dear Nick, I think you're so nice!'

But right now Nick has a major problem. How can he get Rasmus away from here and back to the others? Something must have happened down at the jetty.

The plane never took off, and the motor boats must be important. Something tells Nick the end of this wretched tale has come, and Peters is finished—as finished as he is himself. Nick is satisfied. Everything would be perfect if only Rasmus could get back to his dad now, immediately. A little child can't sit in the forest and watch a person die. Nick wants to spare his friend, but he doesn't know how to go about it. He can't say to him: 'You've got to go now because old Nick's dying and he wants to be alone. Nick wants to lie here completely alone and be glad that you are a free and happy little boy again, who can play with the bow and arrows and the bark boats he made for you.'

No, you can't say that! And now Rasmus is putting his arm around Nick's neck and saying very tenderly:

'Come on, Nick, let's go now! We can go to my daddy!'

'No, Rasmus,' says Nick, with difficulty. 'I'm not going nowhere. I've got to stay here. But you go on your own. I want you to!'

Rasmus sticks out his lower lip.

'Well, I don't want to,' he says, stubbornly. 'I'm waiting till you come with me, so there!'

Nick doesn't answer. He has no strength left, and he doesn't know what to say. Rasmus burrows his nose into Nick's cheek and whispers:

'Because I like you ever so, ever so much!'

And Nick cries. He hasn't cried since he was a child.

But he's crying now. He's crying because he is so tired and because it's the first time anyone has ever said a thing like that to him.

'Fancy that,' he sniffs. 'Fancy you liking an old kidnapper, eh?'

'Well, I think kidnappers are nice,' Rasmus tells him.

Nick gathers the last of his strength.

'Rasmus, you must do what I tell you. You must go to Kalle and Anders and Eva-Lotta. You're going to be a White Rose! I know you want to.'

'Yes, of course I do, but . . .'

'Well, then. Hurry up. I think they're waiting for you.'

'What about you, Nick?'

'Oh, I'll just lie here in the moss, enjoying myself. Have a rest, and listen to the birds chirping.'

'Yes, but . . .' says Rasmus. Then he hears someone calling from far off. Someone calling his name.

'That's my daddy!' says Rasmus, joyfully.

Then Nick cries again, but without a sound this time, his head down in the moss. Sometimes God is good to an old sinner—he doesn't have to worry about Rasmus now. He cries in gratitude, and also because it's hard to say goodbye to the little figure in his grubby dungarees, standing there, hesitating about whether to run to his daddy or stay with Nick.

'Run and tell your dad there's a worn-out old kidnapper lying here in the woods,' says Nick.

Then Rasmus throws his arms around Nick again and sobs:

'You're not a worn-out old kidnapper, Nick!'

Nick lifts his hand slowly and pats Rasmus on the cheek.

'Farewell, little Rasmus,' he whispers. 'Off you go now and be a White Rose. The finest little White Rose . . .'

Rasmus hears his name called again. Sobbing, he stands up, still hesitating and looking down at Nick. Then he leaves. He turns round a couple of times and waves. Nick can't manage to wave back, but he follows the little figure with his blue eyes that are full of tears.

Now there is no more Rasmus. Nick shuts his eyes. He is content now—and tired. It will be good to sleep.

19

'Walter Sigfrid Stanislaus Peters,' the chief inspector said. 'Just the man. At last! Don't you think it was time you were stopped?'

Peters didn't answer.

'Give me a cigarette,' he said impatiently.

Constable Björk walked up to him and stuck a cigarette between his lips.

Peters was sitting on a rock beside the jetty. He was handcuffed. Behind him stood the others: Blom, Svanberg and the foreign pilot.

'Perhaps you know we've been after you for some time,' the chief inspector continued. 'We located the signals from your transmitter two months ago, but you disappeared before we could grab you. Did you get tired of spying, seeing as you turned your hand to kidnapping instead?'

'One's pretty much like the other,' Peters said coldly.

'Perhaps so,' said the chief inspector. 'But now they are both finished, as far as you're concerned.'

'Yes, I guess it's all finished for us now,' said Peters, bitterly. He took a deep puff of his cigarette.

'There is one thing I would really like to know,' he said. 'How did you find out I was here on Kalvön?'

'We didn't until we got here,' said the chief inspector. 'And it was all thanks to an old schoolteacher in Lillköping who just happened to pick up a brief short-wave radio message yesterday evening, sent by our friend Kalle Blomkvist.'

Peters threw Kalle a look full of hate.

'Well, wouldn't you know it,' he said. 'Why didn't I get there two minutes earlier and knock him out properly? Damned kids! It's all their fault, from beginning to end. I'd rather fight the entire Swedish security service than those three.'

The chief inspector walked over to the three White Roses who were sitting on the jetty.

'The security service is lucky to have such first class assistants,' he said.

The three looked down modestly. Kalle thought it wasn't strictly the security services they had helped, but Rasmus.

Peters ground out his cigarette stump with his heel and swore softly and with feeling.

'What are we waiting for?' he snapped. 'Let's get going!'

A small green island among hundreds of others in a blue summer sea. The sun is shining down on the small cabins, on the long jetty and on all the boats moored there, bobbing gently in the waves. High above the tree-tops the gulls soar on their white wings. From time to time one of them dives into the water like a streak of lightning and comes up with a fish in its beak. The little wagtail is still wagging cheekily among the clumps of heather, and the red ants are probably still crawling over the rocks. And perhaps that's how it will continue today, tomorrow and every day until the end of the summer. But no one will know, because no one will be there. Very shortly this island will be deserted and gone from their sight, and they will never, ever see it again.

'I can't see Eva-Lotta's cabin now,' said Kalle.

They were crouched in the stern of the motor boat, staring at the tree-covered island they were leaving behind. They looked back and shuddered. They were relieved to be leaving that green, sunny prison.

Rasmus didn't look back. He sat on his dad's lap and was worried because his dad's face was covered in a shaggy beard. What if it grew so long it got caught in the wheel of his motorbike?

There was something else that bothered him.

'Daddy, why is Nick sleeping in the middle of the daytime? I want him to wake up and talk to me.'

The professor looked in sorrow at the stretcher where Nick was lying unconscious. Would he ever have the chance to thank the man for what he had done for his son? Nick was in a bad way. He didn't look likely to survive. It would be at least two hours before he reached a hospital, and by then it would probably be too late. This truly was a race of life or death. Constable Björk was going as fast as he could, but . . .

'I can't see the jetty any more,' said Eva-Lotta.

'No, and thank goodness for that,' said Kalle. 'But look over there, Anders. There are the rocks we swam from!'

'And our den,' said Anders softly.

'Dens are lots of fun to sleep in, you know, Daddy,' said Rasmus.

Kalle suddenly remembered something he had to tell the professor.

'I hope your motorbike is where we left it,' he said. 'I really hope no one's taken it.'

'We'll come back one day and find out,' said the professor. 'I'm more worried about my documents.'

'Oh, those,' said Kalle, disdainfully. 'I hid them somewhere safe.'

'Now you can tell us where they are,' said Eva-Lotta, keen to find out.

Kalle smiled secretively.

'You'll never guess! In the chest of drawers in the bakery loft, of course!'

Eva-Lotta yelped.

'Have you gone bonkers?' she shouted. 'What if the Reds have swiped them?'

Kalle looked a little concerned at this thought. But then he smiled.

'In that case,' he said, 'We'll swipe them back!'

'Yes!' said Rasmus eagerly. 'We'll make our war cry and swipe them back. I'm going to be a White Rose too, Daddy!'

This sensational piece of news didn't exactly comfort the professor.

'Kalle, you make my hair go grey,' he said. 'Naturally, I'll be grateful to you for as long as I live, but I'll tell you one thing, if those documents are missing . . .'

Constable Björk interrupted him.

'Don't you worry, professor! If Kalle Blomkvist says you'll get your documents, you'll get them!'

'Now Kalvön has disappeared completely,' said Anders, and he spat into the foaming waves churned up by the boat.

'And Nick is just sleeping and sleeping,' said Rasmus.

Their dear old headquarters—nobody ever had better headquarters than the White Roses! The bakery loft is large and roomy, and contains so many interesting things. Just like squirrels gather nuts, through the years the White Roses have gathered together all their prized possessions. Bows and arrows, shields and wooden swords hang on the walls. A trapeze hangs from the ceiling. A table-tennis kit, boxing gloves and old comics are piled in the corners. And against one wall is Eva-Lotta's battered old chest of drawers, where the White Roses keep their secret trophy box. In this very box are the professor's documents. Or rather, were. They've been returned to him now, those wretched documents that have caused so many problems, and from now on they will be kept securely locked in a safety deposit box at the bank.

No, the Reds hadn't taken them. Eva-Lotta needn't have worried.

'Though if we'd known the documents were there, we would have taken them to *our* headquarters instead,' said Sixten, when all the knights of the Red and the White Roses met to go over everything that had happened. They were sitting in the baker's garden, on the grass that sloped down to the little river, and Anders was telling them the whole ghastly story, gesticulating and exaggerating madly.

'It all started when I was hanging from that bush last Thursday night. There hasn't been a minute's peace ever since,' he told them.

'Why does the good stuff always happen to you?' complained Sixten. 'Why couldn't the kidnappers have got there a few minutes earlier, while we were walking past Eklund House?'

'Steady on,' said Eva-Lotta. 'Poor Peters, why should

he have to deal you as well? Isn't a lifetime in prison enough?'

'You're asking for a thump,' said Sixten.

That was the evening after they returned home. A few days had passed since then, and now the White Roses were gathered in the bakery loft. Their leader stood in the middle of the floor, making a pronouncement.

'A noble gentleman and brave warrior will now be granted the title Knight of the White Roses. A fighter whose name is feared far and wide. Rasmus Rasmusson—step forward!'

The feared warrior stepped forward. He might be small and scarcely fearful to look at, but his face burned with the enthusiasm typical of a Knight of the White Roses. He lifted his head to look at his leader. A light gleamed deep inside those dark blue eyes, a light that said Rasmus was about to have something he dearly longed for. Finally, finally, he will be a White Rose!

'Rasmus Rasmusson, you are to raise your right hand and swear a sacred oath. You shall swear to be faithful to the White Roses now and for all your days, not to betray any secrets, and to fight the Red Roses wherever they show their ugly faces.'

'I'll try,' Rasmus said. He raised his hand and began.

'I swear to be a White Rose now and for all my days and to betray every secret wherever they show their ugly faces. Bleeping bellybuttons, I swear!'

'Betray every secret—he'll do that all right,' whispered Kalle to Eva-Lotta. 'I've never known a kid give the game away like he does.'

'Yes, but he's a good boy really,' said Eva-Lotta.

Rasmus looked at his leader expectantly. What was going to happen next?

'You got it wrong,' said Anders. 'But who cares? Kneel, Rasmus Rasmusson.'

Rasmus knelt on the old wooden floorboards. Oh, he was so happy he wanted to kiss them—from now on, this loft would be his headquarters too!

The leader took a sword from the wall.

'Rasmus Rasmusson,' he said. 'As you have now sworn your allegiance to the White Roses with this sacred oath, I hereby dub you Knight of the White Roses.'

He tapped Rasmus on each shoulder with the sword, and Rasmus leapt up from the floor, beaming.

'Am I really a White Rose now?' he asked.

'Whiter than most,' said Kalle.

At that very moment a stone came flying in through the open loft hatch. It landed on the floor with a thud. Anders hurried to pick it up.

'A message from the enemy,' he said, and unfolded the piece of paper wrapped around the stone.

'What have the sweet little Reds got to say this time?' asked Eva-Lotta.

'White Roses, you filthy scum,' read Anders.

You can sniff out important documents from behind bookcases all right, but get your hands on the Great Stonytotem? Never! Becos it is in the lair of the Great Wild Beast whose name shall be a SECRET! But when the Great Wild Beast bites your noses off you'll say half his name, And you make bread from the root. Do you get it, you filthy scum?

'Can we give a war cry now?' asked Rasmus, when the leader had finished.

'Not really. First we've got to think,' said Eva-Lotta. 'Rasmus, what would you say if I bit your nose?'

Eva-Lotta leaned over and nipped him playfully on the tip of his little round nose.

'Hey!' said Rasmus.

'Of course, "hey" is what you say,' said Eva-Lotta.

'And you make bread from wheat,' said Anders. 'Hey-wheat. That sounds barmy enough to have been made up by the Reds.'

'Hey-corn,' said Kalle. 'You've got to have a cornfield to make flour. Haycorn, haycorn—acorn!'

'How on earth did they manage to put the Great Stonytotem in Acorn's kennel?' said Eva-Lotta. 'They must have chloroformed him.'

'What, the Great Stonytotem?' teased Anders.

'No, you twerp, Acorn of course!'

Acorn was the doctor's German shepherd, and he was as bad-tempered as the doctor himself, and that was saying a lot.

'They probably did it when Doctor Hallberg was taking him for a walk,' said Kalle.

'So what do we do now?' asked Eva-Lotta.

They sat on the floor and held a war conference. Rasmus too. He listened with his eyes and ears on stalks—the excitement was beginning at last!

Anders looked at Rasmus and his eyes glittered with an idea. Rasmus had waited so long and so devotedly to be a White Rose that they didn't have the heart to deny him. Although to be honest it was a real nuisance having a little shrimp like him following them around all the time. They would have to try and find a job for him to do, so they could get on with the Wars of the Roses in peace and quiet, without him getting too mixed up in everything.

'You know what, Rasmus?' said Anders. 'Why don't you scamper off to the hospital and see if Acorn is in his kennel!'

'Can I give a war cry if he is?' asked Rasmus.

'Of course you can,' said Eva-Lotta. 'Off you go, now.'

The Whites used a rope for getting in and out of their headquarters, and Rasmus had practised climbing that rope for hours. He couldn't climb up it yet, but he could slide down with no trouble at all, even though it felt stupendously dangerous when he did.

Now he launched himself at the rope and gave one of the wildest war cries that had ever been heard in the baker's garden.

'What a relief,' said Anders, when Rasmus had disappeared. 'Now we can have a serious talk. First thing: find out when Doctor Hallberg usually takes Acorn for a walk. You can do that, Eva-Lotta.'

'Will do,' said Eva-Lotta.

Rasmus tore off towards the hospital. He had been there before to visit Nick, so he knew how to get there. Doctor Hallberg was the senior consultant and his house was right beside the hospital. And right beside the house was Acorn's kennel. 'Private' and 'Beware of the dog' it said on Doctor Hallberg's garden gate. But luckily Rasmus couldn't read, and he marched straight in. Acorn was in his kennel. He growled angrily at Rasmus, and Rasmus came to a halt, troubled. He had misunderstood his mission. He thought it was his responsibility to bring the Great Stonytotem back to their headquarters, but how could he do it when Acorn was growling like that? He looked around for help and to his relief he saw a man coming towards him. And as luck would have it, it was the doctor who had operated on Nick.

Doctor Hallberg was on his way to the hospital when he caught sight of the little knight of the White Roses by Acorn's kennel. Naturally, the doctor didn't know it was a knight standing before him, otherwise he might have been more understanding. As it was, he got very cross, and he walked faster to catch the little rascal red-handed. But Rasmus, who lived in the belief that not only kidnappers were kind but senior consultants too, looked up at the stern face and said:

'Take your dog away for a minute, will you? I've got to get the Great Stonytotem.'

When the doctor didn't immediately do as he was told, Rasmus took him by the hand and pulled him determinedly towards the kennel.

'Please be quick,' he said. 'Because I'm in a stonking hurry.'

'Are you?' said Doctor Hallberg, smiling. He recognized Rasmus now—it was that little lad who had been kidnapped. There had been a lot about him in the newspapers. 'Don't you want to come with me and say hello to Nick?' asked the doctor. 'Yes, but I've got to get the Great Stonytotem first,' said Rasmus firmly.

Nick was told all about the Great Stonytotem. He was allowed to see it too. Proudly, Rasmus stuck it right under his nose. And Rasmus also demonstrated the war cry, so Nick could hear what it sounded like.

'I'm a White Rose now, you see,' said Rasmus. 'I swearded on it a little while ago.' Nick looked at him fondly.

'Yes, and a better one you couldn't hope to find,' he said, happily.

Rasmus patted his hand.

'It's good you're not asleep all the time now, Nick.'

Nick also thought it was good he wasn't asleep. It would still be some time before he could leave hospital, but he knew he would get well again—and what followed, well, he would deal with that somehow. Both the doctor and the professor had promised to help him as much as they could. Nick faced the future calmly.

'And it's good you're not bleeding any more,' said Rasmus, pointing at Nick's hospital gown, that was so clean and white, and didn't have any bloodstains in it.

Nick thought the same. He had never been ill in his life before, and he was full of admiration for the doctors' amazing gadgets and inventions. That blood transfusion, for example—he really wanted to tell Rasmus all about that. Imagine, the doctors took blood from another person and pumped it into him, after he had lost so much of his own out there on Kalvön.

'Did they take it from another kidnapper?' asked Rasmus, who was also amazed at what doctors could think up.

But then he had to hurry. Really, you shouldn't be visiting someone in hospital when you were in the middle of a Roses war. He held the Great Stonytotem tight in his hand and walked towards the door.

'Bye, bye Nick,' he said. 'I'll come back another day.'

And before Nick had time to answer, he was gone.

'Dear little lad,' he said to himself.

Kalle and Anders and Eva-Lotta were still in the bakery loft. Mr Lisander the baker had just been in to offer them freshly baked cinnamon buns.

'You really shouldn't be having any buns at all after the trouble you've caused,' he muttered. 'But never mind.' He patted Eva-Lotta's cheek. 'I'm sure you deserve a few anyway!'

After he had disappeared down to his bakery, a war cry was heard outside. It was the little spy, back from his mission. Making as much noise as an entire army, he charged up the stairs.

'Here,' he said, and threw the Great Stonytotem on the floor.

Kalle, Anders and Eva-Lotta stared at him. Then they stared at the Great Stonytotem. Then they stared at each other. Then they started to laugh.

'The White Roses have got a secret weapon,' said Anders. 'We've got Rasmus.'

'Yes, and the Red Roses might as well give up now,' said Kalle.

Rasmus looked uncertainly from one to the other. They weren't laughing at him, were they? He had done the right thing, surely?

'Did I do well?' he asked anxiously.

Eva-Lotta gave him a little tap on the nose.

'Yes, Rasmus,' she said, laughing. 'You did very, very well!'

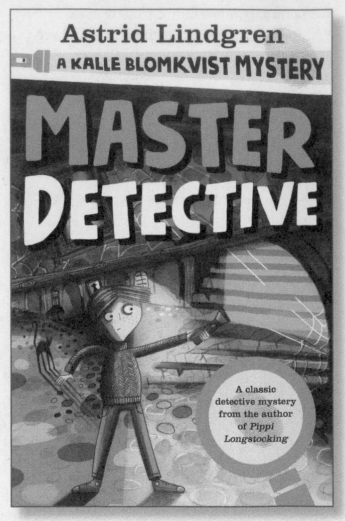

When a mysterious stranger arrives in town, Kalle finds the perfect excuse to start an investigation, one that will draw him and his friends into a thrilling case of theft and deception.

Astrid Lindgren

A KALLE BLOMKVIST MYSTERY

LIVING DANGEROUSLY

A classic detective mystery from the author of *Pippi Longstocking*

One year on from the mysterious case of the missing jewels and it's another summer of sleuthing for Kalle Blomkvist, and this time, there's a murderer on the loose.

Astrid Lindgren

Astrid Lindgren (1907–2002) is one of the most widely-read children's authors in the world. In the course of her life she wrote over 80 books for children, and has sold over 160 million copies worldwide. She once commented, 'I write to amuse the child within me, and can only hope that other children may have some fun that way too.'

Many of Astrid Lindgren's stories are based upon her memories of childhood and they are filled with lively and unconventional characters. Perhaps the best known is *Pippi Longstocking*, first published in Sweden in 1945. It was an immediate success, and was published in England in 1954.

Awards for Astrid Lindgren's writing include the prestigious Hans Christian Andersen Award and the International Book Award. In 1989 a theme park dedicated to her—*Astrid Lindgren Värld*—was opened in her home town of Vimmerby. When she passed away in 2002, the Swedish Government founded The Astrid Lindgren Memorial Award (ALMA) in her honour. It is the world's largest prize for children's and young adult literature.

ALSO BY ASTRID LINDGREN

A Kalle Blomkvist Mystery:
Master Detective

A Kalle Blomkvist Mystery:
Living Dangerously

Seacrow Island

Mio's Kingdom

Ronia the Robber's Daughter

The Brothers Lionheart

Pippi Longstocking
Pippi Longstocking Goes Aboard
Pippi Longstocking in the South Seas

Karlson on the Roof
Karlson Flies Again
The World's Best Karlson

Emil's Clever Pig
Emil and the Great Escape
Emil and the Sneaky Rat

Lotta Says 'No!'
Lotta Makes a Mess

The Children of Noisy Village
Happy Times in Noisy Village
Nothing But Fun in Noisy Village

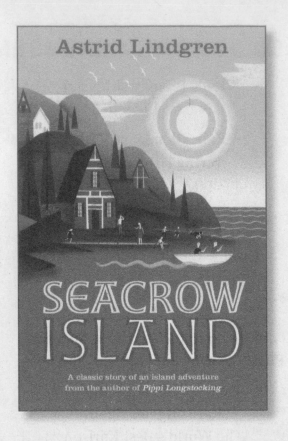

Astrid Lindgren

SEACROW
ISLAND

A classic story of an island adventure
from the author of *Pippi Longstocking*

The day the Melkerson family arrive on Seacrow Island,
it's a bit of a shock to their system. It's so quiet there—
none of the shops and bustle they're used to. And the
cottage they've rented for the summer is a little bit . . .
well . . . *basic*. But what Seacrow Island does have is
woods to wander in, fish to catch, boats to sail in, and all
kinds of animals. And before long they find it has even
more important things too—adventure, fun, exploration,
friends . . . Perhaps it's going to be leaving that's the
really hard thing?

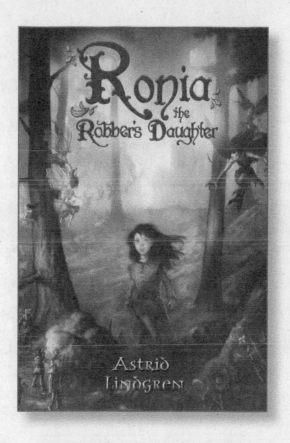

High on a mountainside, a band of robbers live in a great
fortress. Ronia, the daughter of the robber chieftain,
roams the forest but she must beware the grey dwarfs
and wild harpies. When she befriends Birk, the son of
her father's greatest enemy, it causes uproar. Ronia and
Birk can no longer be friends—unless they do something
drastic. Like running away . . . Suddenly they are fending
for themselves in the woods, but how will they survive
when winter comes? And will Ronia's father ever accept
her friendship with Birk, so they can go home?

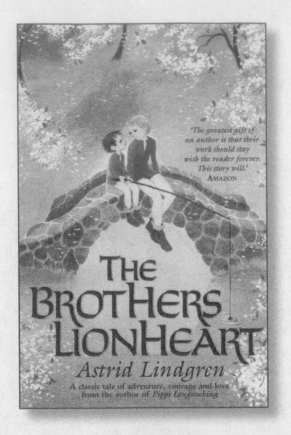

'The greatest gift of an author is that their work should stay with the reader forever. This story will.'
AMAZON

THE BROTHERS LIONHEART

Astrid Lindgren

A classic tale of adventure, courage and love from the author of *Pippi Longstocking*

'In Nangiyala you have adventures from morning till evening...' That's what brave Jonathan Lionheart tells his sick younger brother, Karl. So when both boys tragically die and are united in the 'land beyond the stars', they know their adventures are just beginning...

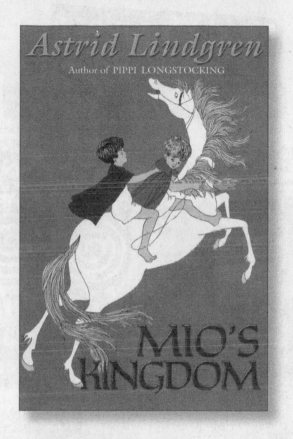

*Did you hear the news about a boy who disappeared? No
one knows what happened to him . . . except me.* Young
Karl leaves behind his unhappy life as an unwanted
foster child to escape to Farawayland. There, he learns
that his true name is Mio, and that he is the son of the
King. But the kingdom is under threat. The evil Sir Kato
terrorizes the land, and it has been foretold that Mio is
the only one who can defeat him . . .

Ready for more great stories? Try one of these...